OPERATION
TROPICAL
AFFAIR

a Poppy McVie adventure

OPERATION
TROPICAL
AFFAIR

KIMBERLI A. BINDSCHATEL

Turning Leaf · Traverse City, MI

Published by Turning Leaf Productions, LLC.
Traverse City, Michigan

www.PoppyMcVie.com
www.KimberliBindschatel.com

Print ISBN-13:9780996189026
Print ISBN-10:0996189025

This is a work of fiction. Names, characters, businesses, places, events and incidents are either the products of the author's imagination or used in a fictitious manner. Any resemblance to actual persons, living or dead, or actual events is purely coincidental.

Thank you for purchasing this book and supporting an indie author.

For Marie, my Muse

And to the brave men and women of the U.S.F.W.S. and their counterparts around the globe who dedicate their lives to save animals from harm. Their courage and commitment is nothing short of inspiring.

May their efforts not be in vain.

The greatness of a nation can be judged by the way its animals are treated.

~Mahatma Gandhi

OPERATION TROPICAL AFFAIR

a Poppy McVie adventure

CHAPTER 1

I knew they'd come for her. The poor thing. Wandering in unknown territory trying to shake a disorienting drugged-out haze. She was easy prey for a couple of two-bit rednecks. Goes to show how things are bass ackwards in this world.

Well, they weren't going to get away with it. Not on my watch.

Honey Bear—as she'd been christened by Sally Newberry, the second grader who'd won the naming contest run by *The Mining Gazette*—had been caught rummaging through the trash cans of some downstater who didn't know any better than to throw her chicken bones into a black plastic bag and set it right out on her back porch. Might as well hang a neon welcome sign. It was the bear, of course, who needed to be *rehabilitated*. Dubbed a "trouble" bear, she'd been trapped, tranquilized, poked and prodded, then released yesterday afternoon here on the north side of the refuge. Now she was an easy target.

The sun hadn't poked up over the horizon yet and there they were. Just as I thought. The Lawson boys. Coming down the two-track in their souped up purple Geo Tracker. It was outfitted with a state-of-the-art antennae mounted on the roof, makeshift kennels built into the back, and two greasy haired, grinning idiots inside. The true genius of their bear poaching contraption was the blue tick hound dog straddling the hood, his collar chained to an eye hook mounted where a hood ornament would go, his long ears flapping in the wind. This way, his nose was right out front to catch bear scent. I shook my head. Rednecks. I aimed the video camera and pushed the record button.

The dog's name was Brutus. I'd met him a few weeks ago when I'd pulled them over and demanded they take him off the hood. They were just outside the refuge and claimed they were training the dogs for the legal season. Not my jurisdiction, but I couldn't help it. The heat from the engine could burn his paws and being chained to a moving vehicle was dangerous, not to mention absurd. They promised to glue some carpeting up there, give 'im something to grip, they'd said. Assured me that'd do the trick. Jackasses.

Roy, my SAC, (that's special-agent-in-charge), told me to choose my battles. Hell, it's not illegal and besides, we have bigger fish to fry, he'd said after he'd eased out of his pickup and went through his usual routine of tugging at his belt, pulling up his pants, first on one side, then the other, then sauntered over to stand beside me and ask what was the matter.

At first, I didn't know what to think of Roy. Michigan's Upper Peninsula was my first duty station and Roy the experienced officer I was assigned to do field training under for my first forty-four weeks on duty. Soon enough I'd realized Roy's kinda lovable in a grandpappy kind of way, what with the green flannel jacket he wears everyday and the old red plaid Stormy Kromer hat covering his bare head, ear flaps up in the summer, down over his ears in the winter. He's got that easy, laid back disposition that makes you feel like time's an illusion and tomorrow's just as good a day as ever to do whatever it is you might be pondering doing.

I got him some snazzy suspenders for his birthday. He gave me a half-grin and a genuine confused look, asked whatever in the world I'd done that for, the belt he had worked just fine. I wasn't sure if I'd made a serious faux pas, or as they say in *da* U.P., if I'd *stepped in it*. There was a long, awkward moment, the kind which I've come to accept as a common reaction to me, before he'd chuckled and snapped on the new suspenders. Course he still adjusts the pants in the same old routine.

Brutus let out a yowl and the little Jeep-wannabe came to a halt. He'd caught Honey Bear's scent.

I shoved the last of my granola bar in my mouth and hunkered down in my blind. I was sure the Lawson boys were planning to dart Honey Bear and sell her live to an illegal bear bile farmer where she'd spend the rest of her life barely conscious, crammed into a cage no larger than her outstretched body to restrict her movement, a metal catheter implanted into her gall bladder to withdraw a continuous supply of bile. The cruel practice causes excruciating misery for the bear. But poachers don't care. Bear bile sells like liquid gold. 250ccs fetches around US $1000 in China to those who believe in traditional medicine. They say it's a cure-all for hepatitis, hemorrhoids, hangovers, and chronic diarrhea. Maybe it is. But torturing a bear to get it, well, I'd take on the PLA to stop it if I could. Right now, in my corner of the world, I'd have given my right eye to see these bastards fry, but sending them to prison would have to do. I just had to bust them first.

And today, that's just what I was going to do.

The boys got out of the car. The dogs were going ape shit, yipping with excitement. I had about ten seconds to call it in. Roy answered the phone right away. "What now, McVie?"

"Listen, I'm in the northwest unit, off the Old State Road. The Lawson boys just pulled up in their hound wagon."

"What the hell are you up to?"

"They released Honey Bear yesterday."

Roy sighed. I could tell he was rubbing his temples, like he always does. "You been out there all night?"

Roy had an annoying habit of asking the obvious.

"Listen to me now, girl. Don't you go underestimating them boys. Out there alone in them woods, that badge ain't gonna protect you."

"What good is this badge if I can't protect the animals?"

I tried to pull the phone from my ear to hang up, but it was stuck in my hair, all matted and tangled with a gob of pine sap. Roy was still yammering on the other end. "You wait for me to get out there." I yanked it free, punched the end button, and put on my USFWS hat. At least I tried. Somebody had the bright idea to require us to wear these things. Whoever it was has never tried to tame my mop. I shoved my ponytail through the opening in the back and called it good. I was ready.

Bear hunting with dogs works like this. The dogs catch the scent. The hunter (if you call it hunting) sends his pack of dogs to chase down the bear, tree the poor thing, then the men track their prey using GPS to the location sent by the remote contraption on the dog's collar. The dogs might run for several miles before they corner the bear. So the Lawson boys will tool along in the little Geo, watching a blip on a tiny screen until they get the signal that the lead dog has stopped. Then they'll saunter over to the bear, all puffed up and proud of themselves, and shoot the helpless creature out of the tree.

Unfortunately, in Michigan, this is perfectly legal. In fact, letting your dogs chase a bear in the off-season, terrorizing it for training and practice, is also legal. Darting a bear and capturing it live isn't.

As my grandpa always said, come hell or high water, I was going to catch them doing it.

The problem was, they had the advantage of a dedicated GPS unit. If I followed them, they'd see me and bail, claiming they were just out letting their dogs run. I had one choice. Do it the old-fashioned way: keep up with the dogs.

The good thing is a pack of hound dogs will yip and yap, making a ruckus as they race after a bear. When they close in on their prey, they start baying, a low bawling that can be heard from a distance. The bad thing is they can run about twenty miles per hour. Good thing I wore my wilderness running boots.

The kennel doors were flung open, Brutus was unchained, and

the pack took off through the woods, yapping with excitement. I waited for the boys to latch the kennels closed and mosey to their seats then drive off before I left the blind. I strapped on my running pack and slipped my hand into the strap on the video camera. With a deep breath, I touched the bracelet at my wrist. *I know you're with me, Dad.* And I took off after them.

The dogs headed southwest and kept a steady pace for about fifteen minutes, gaining distance ahead of me. Twice, I slipped in the mud on wet leaves, but for the most part I managed to keep upright and moving forward. Then their vocalizations changed. They were close to the bear now and had her on the run.

I slid down the edge of a ravine, sprinted up the other side, barreled through a patch of brambles, and tripped and fell flat on my stomach. The video camera went tumbling. I got up and shook it off. I needed a moment to regain my bearings.

The pack had headed into an old logging area where the pines grew in rows. I picked up the camera, made sure it was still working, and sprinted down a fairway until I ran out of steam. I bent over, my hands on my thighs, my chest heaving. These dogs were fit. After I caught my breath, I continued on. They weren't far off. Must have her treed already, I realized. *I'm coming Honey Bear!* I approached with caution in case I was wrong; a terrified bear wasn't someone I wanted to stumble upon.

I homed in on the yowls. They came from an open area covered with moss and grass that had been trampled by deer bedding down overnight. Sure enough, on the far side was Honey Bear. She'd shinnied up an old oak tree, all four paws clamped on. She was grunting and growling while the dogs whined and scratched at the base of the tree. Brutus had his head tilted back, howling for his masters.

I quickly scanned the area. I needed a place to hide. My own prey would be along soon. My best option was a small spruce pine on the edge of the clearing. I set the video camera in the crook of a branch, pointing toward Honey Bear, double checked it was recording—I didn't want any mistakes on this one—then crawled beneath the pine boughs and checked my phone. No cell service here. Using the handheld radio was too risky; anyone could be listening in. I texted the GPS coordinates to Roy, hoping a text would make it through, then hunkered down to wait.

It seemed like an eternity. Poor Honey Bear was frothing at the mouth. For successful bear poachers, they sure were slow. There was no doubt, though, that's what they were. Word around town was, last winter, they'd showed up at the Buckhorn Bar with brand new snowmobiles, acting like big shots, buying all their buddies Budweisers and running their mouths about hitting it big time. They were tight lipped about details, though. Come spring they had new four-runners and shiny new Remington shotguns. It didn't take a seasoned Special Agent to figure out they were doing something illegal. Since they had no common sense and couldn't hold a regular job, it wasn't hard to surmise they were making money on the only thing they were good at. Poaching.

My father and I had run into poachers a few times over the years. Spend enough time in the wilderness and it's bound to happen. I'd rather face down a tiger than an angry, gun-toting poacher. The image of my father, facing down a poacher was too much—I heard their voices. Then I caught sight of them ambling into the clearing. Jed, the longer haired one, held the GPS tracker in his left hand, and—*I knew it!*—a dart gun in his right. His cousin Larry was right behind him, a shotgun slung over his shoulder. They both wore Carhartt coats, blue jeans, and the requisite baseball caps, always sporting either some beer logo or a silhouette of a woman, the kind that commonly adorns the mud flaps of an eighteen wheeler. I'd seen them all.

I could arrest them right now for carrying a loaded shotgun with the dogs off-season, but the penalty was a slap on the wrist. No. I wanted them for poaching a live bear.

Jed nodded to his cousin, a shit-eating grin on his face.

Leaving Brutus on point, they called off the other five dogs and tied them to nearby trees. Then Jed took the shotgun from Larry, handed him the dart gun, and grumbled something I couldn't quite make out.

Larry beamed with pride.

I looked up at Honey Bear. My heart clenched. *Sorry girl, I have to let them do it. It's the only way. You'll be all right.*

Larry raised the gun and pulled the trigger. The dart flew wide and stuck in a tree limb low and to the right.

Jed yanked the dart gun from Larry's hands. "Gimme that, you dumbass," he said. "We don't got none to waste." He shoved the shotgun at him. "Hold that."

Jed zeroed in and let the dart fly. It struck its target. Honey Bear flinched and dug in with her claws. Soon her head started to droop and she slid halfway down the tree trunk, ripping bark off in tiny strips, until her claws let loose and she flopped to the ground with a thud. Larry let out a hoot.

"That's how it's done!" Jed shouted and gave Larry a high five.

The dogs bounced around, barking themselves hoarse, yanking to the end of their ropes.

Jed leaned the dart gun against the tree and while Larry tied up Brutus, he took some twine from his pocket and hogtied the bear. He slipped a muzzle around her mouth, cinched it tight, then punched something into his cell phone. Texting the GPS coordinates, I assumed. He wasn't stupid enough to drag this bear out of here right now, with the dogs and the dart gun. Someone else was the pickup crew.

I crawled out from under my tree, brushed off the pine needles, and straightened my hat. Then I walked right up behind the cocky bastards. "Howdy boys." Jed spun around. Larry's head bobbed over his shoulder, his mouth hanging wide open. He blinked twice, his eyeballs bulging like a bullfrog in a murky swamp. He wasn't sure if I was real or an apparition.

He still had the shotgun slung over his shoulder. I kept my weapon holstered. Provoking an armed idiot wasn't a good idea. I was glad it was Larry who had the firearm, though. He wasn't a killer. He'd hesitate. Besides, his aim sucked.

Jed, the smarter of the two, screwed up his face, trying to figure out how I'd gotten all the way out here in the middle of the woods. He spit a glob of black goo out the side of his crusty lip. "Who the hell are you?"

"Special Agent McVie. You're under arrest."

"Really?" He smirked and glanced at his cousin. "And who's gonna arrest me?"

Cousin Larry's eyes darted back and forth, eyeing every tree another agent might be lurking behind. "Yeah, who?" he muttered.

"Wait, I know you," Jed said as he took a step closer to me.

Good. Keep coming closer.

"You that new duck cop. Pippa, ain't it?"

"Special Agent McVie. Now step back. Turn around, put your hands up, and lace your fingers behind your neck."

"Pippa, huh?" said Larry. "Like that princess a' England. Dude, she's hot."

"Shut up, Larry." Jed took another step toward me.

That's it. Keep coming.

"Now what you doin' way out here all by yerself?" His eyes traveled down to my waist and back up, settling on my chest. "Ain't it kinda dangerous? A sweet young thing, all alone in the woods?"

He took another step closer, just beyond my arm's length. He wore steel-toed boots. That was to his advantage. And he stood a foot taller and had at least a hundred pounds on me, too. But his Carhartt coat would restrict his movement. I looked up at him. "I can take care of myself. Now turn around."

He grinned. "You hear that, Larry." He turned his head to spit. At least he was that polite.

Larry scratched his neck. "Jed, I think we oughta just go."

"Well, Larry, that's the thing. We can't *just go*. She seen us."

I nodded. "It's true, Larry. I did."

Honey Bear moaned and tried to get up, licking her lips like an old drunk. *Hold on, Honey Bear, just a bit longer.* I turned my gaze back to Jed. "You see, Larry," I said, my eyes locked with Jed's. "That beautiful bear is going to stay right here where she belongs, in the wild. And you and your cousin are the ones headed for a cage."

"Sheee-at," Jed said. "Ain't you a feisty little thing?" His toned changed. "Larry, go get the dart gun. We gonna have us some fun."

"Larry, don't you move a muscle," I said, my eyes still on Jed. I could handle these two, but if they got a dart in me...

Jed howled with laughter. "Woohoo, this is gonna be fun!" he shouted. Then he made a mistake. He took one step closer and grabbed me by the shoulder. I planted my foot, flung my arm up over his, and dropped. His elbow made a crack as it broke. *That's for Honey Bear, you son of a bitch.* I butted him in the back of his knee and took him down. He landed on his belly, bellowing like a pig in heat. I rammed my boot into the small of his back, grabbed his broken arm at the wrist, twisted it to meet his other wrist, and slapped a twist-tie around both.

"Holy mother!" said Larry. He tossed his shotgun to the ground and took off running.

I kept my boot rammed in Jed's back while I unclipped my radio from my belt. "Suspect is on foot, heading north-northwest from my location."

"Yeah," was all I heard. I looked up to see Roy at the edge of the clearing. Larry was backing away from him. He tripped and fell on his ass. "Got him," Roy yelled with a wave.

I leaned over and whispered to Jed. "Tell me who you're selling these bears to."

"Screw you," he growled and spat.

I rolled him over, sat him up, and just as he drew in a breath, I smacked him on the back. He coughed and hacked.

"How's that chew taste?" I asked.

"Bitch, I ain't telling you nothin."

"That's okay," I said. "Something tells me he's on his way. We'll just wait here for him." Jed closed his eyes and put his head down.

Roy had Larry handcuffed and leaning against a tree. He stomped toward me.

"What the hell were you thinking?" he snapped. "I told you to wait."

"I had to catch them in the act."

Roy closed his eyes and rubbed his temples with his left hand. He looked over at the bear, then down at Jed who was moaning, his right arm twisted at the wrong angle. "What am I gonna do with you?"

I clenched my teeth together. I knew when to keep my mouth shut. Well…most of the time. Roy shook his head and walked away.

I went to Honey Bear, knelt beside her, and stroked her head between her ears. *You'll be all right. Just sleep for now. It will all be over soon.*

Roy had gotten about four paces before he turned around. "While you've been out here galavanting around, the CO's been trying to get you on the phone. I didn't want to use the radio."

"What's he want?"

"Dunno. Said to call right away."

"As in right now?" Our CO, head of the Midwest region, was headquartered in Minnesota, an hour behind. "He's up early." I had to walk about two hundred yards to get a signal. Three missed calls. *Crap.* I punched the call back button. "This is Special Agent McVie, I—"

"Hold the line," I was told. Then seconds later, "McVie?"

"Yes sir, what's—"

"Pack a bag and get to the Detroit airport by six p.m. You're booked on a flight to Georgia."

"Georgia?" The federal law enforcement training center, FLETC, is in Georgia. "I just had my FLETC training. Wait, did you say six p.m.? But, sir, Detroit's an eight hour drive from here."

"Yeah, you better get moving. Leave your badge and firearm with Roy."

"My badge, sir?" Why would he ask me to leave my badge? "Have I done something wrong?"

"Temporarily reassigned."

"Reassigned?" I'd been a field agent for only four months. I was still doing field training. This was unheard of. This couldn't be good. "Where?"

"Uh—" There was a long pause. "Actually, I don't know."

"What do you mean, you don't know?" *What the hell is going on?*

"I was told to tell you to wear civilian clothes."

"I'm not sure I understand."

He huffed. "It's above my pay grade. Alls I know is you've been specifically requested. That means they ain't askin."

This wasn't making any sense. I glanced back toward Roy and the Lawson boys. "I can't leave now. I just busted a couple poachers taking a live bear. We've got to stake out—"

"Roy can handle that."

"Yeah, but Roy—"

"Poppy." He sighed. "Just get your ass on the damn plane."

Chapter 2

As I exited the jetway in Atlanta, I ran smack into an airport employee holding a paper plate with McVie scribbled across the back. Nice. I followed the young man but started to get the feeling I was getting punked, like I was being walked onto the set of a seventies horror movie—the long, confusing corridors, the lone flickering fluorescent bulb, all the closed, unmarked doors.

He finally came to a halt in front of what looked like a broom closet. Porn movie then? He gestured for me to go on in. "Thanks?" I managed.

I gripped the door knob and flung open the door. "Hi, I'm Poppy McVie."

A balding man in a crumpled white shirt and a tired striped tie looked up from his desk and frowned. His left hand lay atop a briefcase that looked like it had been issued during the Vietnam War. It was crammed full of manila folders. Definitely from headquarters.

"Poppy!"

I turned. It was Mr. Strix, my favorite instructor from FLETC. What was he doing here? He bowled me over with a bear hug. This was new. "I'm so glad you were available," he said. He gestured toward the stuffed shirt. "This is Stan Martin, head of Special Operations."

I snapped to attention and glanced back to Mr. Strix, my

eyebrows raised in a did-you-just-say-what-I-think-you-said question. The head of Special Ops? Mr. Strix gave me a quick wink.

"It's nice to meet you, sir," I said. *Holy crap, Special Ops! Special Ops! Okay, calm. Stay calm.* I pasted a professional smile on my face—not too wide, no teeth.

Mr. Martin was staring at me with that look. The oh-my-god-she's-just-a-girl look. He frowned. I frowned. The thing is, I'm five foot two and all of one hundred and four pounds. I have unruly red hair and freckles and in high school, kids called me Pippity-Poppity-Poo, as in Pippi Longstocking, the precocious Swedish children's book character who has no manners and—this is my favorite part—can lift her horse with one hand. Not exactly the moniker of which a teenage girl dreams.

In college, I wore fake glasses for a semester, the kind with clear lenses, thinking they'd make me appear older, more sophisticated. Damn things gave me headaches.

Now, at age twenty-four, on looks alone, I could probably pass for Pippi's older sister. I've learned to accept people's reactions to me. Well, mostly. Okay, sometimes. When I'm in the mood. Like when I'm meeting the head of the organization of which I've dreamed of working since—well, forever.

"Why don't you have a seat?" said Mr. Strix, his hand on my back, gently guiding me toward a chair. I dropped my duffle next to the door and sat down. He perched on the side of the desk and adjusted his thick round glasses. "We don't have a lot of time, so why don't we get right to it."

"Yes, sir," I smiled and turned to Mr. Martin. "So I'm being promoted to Special Ops?"

Mr. Martin harrumphed. Actually harrumphed. *Oops. Apparently that wasn't the thing to ask.* He crossed his arms and shook his head. I looked to Mr. Strix for help. He cleared his throat and put on a smile. "Temporarily reassigned. An Ops team is in need of a, well they need some help, an agent with your—" He sat up straighter. "Unique skills and talents."

"Okay," I said. What else could I say? No one knew what I was capable of better than Mr. Strix.

Mr. Martin closed the briefcase. "Jim, I'm not sure she's—"

Strix held up his hand. "Now Stan, you asked for my recommendation. Poppy is as bright as a whip. She was top of her class." He beamed with pride. "I have every confidence in her—"

"I got the resumé," Mr. Martin said. "But for Special Ops, an agent needs—"

"Balls," I said.

Their heads snapped in my direction.

"That's your concern, right?" I sat up straighter and looked him in the eye. "What exactly do you need me to do?"

Mr. Martin regarded me with skeptical eyes for a long moment. His lips puckered and unpuckered. Twice. Finally, he sighed and said, "We're nine months into a long-term investigation." From the briefcase he plucked a folder, flipped it open, and handed me a photo. "Our target: George Hillman. An ex-pat living in Costa Rica. He sells legal species for the pet trade, frogs, snakes, whatever. We know he's the contact for the sale of some exotics, CITES class I and II species, but the offer to sell always comes anonymously, so we can't pin it on him. More importantly, we think he's the connection to the kingpin of shark fin exports. Shark fins are big business and the Costa Rican government has asked for our help."

I knew a bit about shark finning. In a few short years, fishermen had decimated ninety percent of the shark population off the coast of Costa Rica. The black market price for shark fins soared up to $700 a kilogram. Shark meat, which is legal to harvest, has remained inexpensive and, therefore, not worth carrying for the fishermen. To maximize the space in their holds, they'd begun hacking off a shark's fins while they had it on the hook, then tossing the still-breathing creature back into the sea, unable to swim. It's heinous.

"This George is the target for shark finning? You said he

deals in exotics for the pet trade."

Mr. Martin shrugged. "We know he's connected. But he's slippery. We don't know much else."

"What *do* you know?"

His eyebrows narrowed. Lips puckered.

Oops. "I mean, what else can you tell me?"

Mr. Strix shifted his position on the desk. His head pivoted around so he could see me through the narrow vision of his glasses. "Poppy, you must understand, the guys on the ground are undercover. It can be risky to make contact with headquarters and when they do, they don't always have time to tell us much."

"So what are their assignments then?"

"That's the thing," said Strix. "They—"

"This is an elite team. The best of the best. I don't give these men assignments," said Mr. Martin with impatience. "I give them objectives and they work independently." He closed the folder and frowned. "You'll be briefed when you get there by the SAC, Joe Nash."

Joe Nash! Joe Nash was a legend. A super legend. He practically wrote the book on Special Operations. In as indifferent a voice as I could muster, I said, "I heard he has his years in for retirement."

"He does, but he says he won't file until he nails this guy."

I nodded. I could relate.

"He's posing as a rich collector. We have another man on the ground, Special Agent Dalton." I hadn't heard of him. "He's a buyer. Then there's a third agent on the case, Special Agent Tom García. We've had no contact from him in weeks." He looked concerned.

"What was his objective?" I asked. They were throwing a lot at me at once, probably to see if I could keep it straight.

Mr. Martin said, "He was working the poaching side, trying to identify the buncher." He paused. "A buncher is—"

"I know. The middle-man. He buys from the poachers, tends

the inventory, then sells to the smuggling kingpin."

Mr. Martin gave me a respectful nod. He handed me a post card. "His last correspondence." The image was of a palapa bar on the beach called The Toucan. On the back García had scribbled a message: *Having a great time. Have my sights set on a beautiful butterfly. Paco.*

"What's that mean?"

Mr. Martin shrugged. "Dunno. Butterflies are a big black market species. When you talk to Nash, give him the info. Maybe it makes sense to him."

I tried to read the postmarked date. "When did you get this?"

"Two weeks ago. Nothing since. It could be he's too deep to make contact."

Mr. Strix shifted to the edge of the desk. "It's a dangerous operation, Poppy. When you work Special Ops, you're on your own."

I sat back. I could handle that. In fact, I preferred it. "Is this typical protocol? To bring in another agent right in the middle of an investigation?"

The two men looked at each other, tight-lipped. Mr. Martin leaned back in his chair and crossed his arms. "Undercover work isn't like you've read in your textbooks, young lady."

Young lady? I could feel my teeth involuntarily clenching together.

Strix drew in a breath. "Poppy, listen. This op is vital. We've had very short notice to find someone, the right someone, to send in." He leaned forward and adjusted his glasses. "I believe that someone is you."

"So how do I fit in?"

Mr. Strix grinned as if he were about to hand me a winning lottery ticket. "You're going to choose your own pet monkey."

I looked to Mr. Martin, then back to him. "I've always wanted a monkey?" The Barenaked Ladies tune started playing in my head.

Mr. Martin picked up a pencil and tapped it on the folder. The beat didn't match the rhythm of the tune in my head and it was aggravating. "You'll be partnered with Special Agent Dalton. His cover is the owner of a chain of pet stores in Texas." He handed me a business card with the info. "He spends about ten days in Costa Rica once a month. He's built a rapport with George and recently hinted at wanting to buy class II species. Specifically," he cocked his head to the side, "he mentioned how his wife wants her own pet monkey."

He paused, waiting for my reaction. The fluorescent tube above, as if on cue, flickered and hummed. As he had said, Special Ops is an elite group. Those guys were seasoned agents. The legendary Joe Nash was in his late sixties. Thinning hair, arthritis. Dalton must have been about the same. *Probably has dentures.*

"So I'm the trophy wife," I said. *The things I do for animals.* I held out my hand for the folder. "How long do I have to study my cover?"

Mr. Martin put out his hands, palms up. "That's it."

I looked to Mr. Strix. "What do you mean, that's it? How do I make contact? Where do I go?"

He reached into a sack that had been tucked beside the desk and produced a wide-brimmed straw hat and a god-awful handbag—gold lamé with a giant buckle studded with sparkling bling. It was large enough to carry a poodle. "Seriously?" I asked.

He examined the handbag, innocently perplexed by my reaction. "It's my wife's," he said, as if that made it unquestioningly perfect.

I zipped my lip.

Mr. Martin looked at his watch. "Your flight's in one hour. You connect through Dallas where you'll switch to first class." He eyed my duffle. "Make sure you pick up a new carry-on bag that's appropriate to your cover."

Mr. Strix took my hand and slipped a diamond the size of

Montana onto my finger. I shook my head. "Whoa."

"Yeah, well, you'll be running with the big spenders. Besides,"—he gave me a wink—"Brittany's worth it."

"You've got to be kidding. Brittany?"

Mr. Martin harrumphed again. "This from a girl named Poppy."

My eyebrows stretched upward so far my eyeballs hurt. In a soothing voice, which from anyone else would seem condescending, Mr. Strix said, "Dalton had to pick something. He didn't know at the time we'd be sending someone in."

I tried to smile, wondering if the next trick he'd pull from the bag was a voucher for a boob job.

"Dalton will be at the airport in San José to pick you up. He'll be wearing tan slacks and a light blue polo shirt. Make sure you wear this hat." He plopped it on my head.

I flipped through the folder again. "Where's a picture of Special Agent Dalton?"

The two men looked at each other, blank faced.

This was starting to feel like some kind of back room, cold war, clandestine mission. Flick the lighter twice, knock once. It was going to be fun. I wanted to rattle off a *I'm your Natasha* in my best Russian accent. Instead, I said, "It's all right."

Mr. Martin leaned forward on the desk. "Listen, I know this situation isn't ideal. But Jim assures me you're up for it." He set his jaw. "You need to understand the serious nature of the op you're walking into. One mistake could mean your life or the life of a fellow agent. Got it?"

I took off the hat. (It was going to be a full-on job to get my mop to fit in that thing.) "I got it."

"I mean it, Agent McVie." He paused for a beat. Then huffed and shook his head. He glared at Mr. Strix. "I hope I don't regret this." He turned his glare on me. "Rule number one of undercover work: always keep your cover. The thing is, undercover work is like improv. Don't take anything personally. You've gotta roll with it. You two are newlyweds, so smooch it up. You never know who might be watching."

"I understand, sir." I had the urge to ask if I should pick up some Viagra on the way, but I was already pushing my luck and Mr. Martin didn't seem to have much of a sense of humor.

"Rule number two: tell as few lies as possible. Makes it easier to keep things straight. If you liked Barbies when you were seven, then Brittany liked Barbies when she was seven. The key is to be yourself, to act natural. Got it?"

I nodded. "Barbies. Got it."

"Three: if something doesn't feel right, don't proceed. Walk away. Be patient. You don't want to push a relationship. Better to take another day than to blow it. And four: if you suspect you've been made, get the hell out of there. Notify your SAC right away."

"Yes, sir."

"If you get the chance to meet George, be cautious. He's likely going to test you. He'll scrutinize everything you say and do."

"George. Test me. Got it."

He stared for a long moment as though it were his last chance to change his mind.

"Is that all, sir?"

He heaved a sigh. "Good luck."

Mr. Strix rose to his feet. "I'll walk you out."

I slung the rich-bitch bag over my shoulder and gave Mr. Stan Martin a nod.

After two right turns and three to the left, Mr. Strix handed me a cell phone. "A Michigan number is programmed under Mom. It will transfer to me. Call if you need anything."

"Michigan?" I asked, but as the word came out of my mouth I realized. "No Texas accent. I grew up in Michigan. Got it." I stopped and turned to him. "Thanks," I said.

He smiled.

"Has there been any news on my dad's case?"

He shook his head. "I'm sorry. Nothing."

I walked a few more feet, turned and—nope. I was going to let it go.

He lifted his glasses to rub his eyes and sighed. "What is it?"

"Nothing, sir." I turned to continue on.

He gently grabbed my arm. "It's Special Ops. That's what you've always wanted."

"Yes, sir. Thank you for recommending me, sir."

"I was glad to do it. You'll make me proud. Just promise me you'll be careful."

We continued on, another left turn. I stopped again. "The wife? Really? I was *specifically requested* because they need a woman? That's it?"

"Listen to me." He took me by the shoulders like my dad used to do to make me face him. "It's an opportunity. Take it." He gave me a hopeful smile. "When you get there, listen to your SAC, follow protocol, and I'm confident, in no time, they'll see your potential." He gave me another hug. "Trust me, Poppy."

I gave him a smile of thanks and winked. "You can call me Brittany."

Juan Santamaría International Airport in San José, Costa Rica is the second busiest airport in Central America. This was an advantage. Even someone I knew, like my own husband, might be easily overlooked in the bustling crowd.

At Customs and Immigration, I presented my new passport. Under my mug was the name Brittany Katherine Fuller. It even had my actual birthday, April 3, 1990. Someone was really thinking when they tucked in an immunization card with an emergency contact: my husband of three months, John Randolf Fuller.

I ran through some memorization routines. *Hi, I'm Brittany, John's wife. So nice to meet you, George. This is my husband,*

John. John, John. I need to go to the John with John. John the
baptist. John Lennon. Johnny. Johnny be good. Johnny Depp.
Oooooh yeah. Johnny Depp. I could be married to Johnny
Depp.

I couldn't think of any thing else to prepare. During my
flight from Detroit, I had rummaged through the handbag and
found a pack of gum, a tin of aspirin, two emery boards, several
maxi pads, a bottle of hand lotion (half used), a mini-pack of
tissues, a pair of cheesy, goggle lens sunglasses, and a change
purse that looked like it was handmade by someone's grandma.
Everything a girl could need and all courtesy, no doubt, of
Mrs. Strix. I'd have to remember to send her a thank-you note.
Without the typical items, I was at risk of someone realizing
that stunning fashion accessory was a prop. There was no time
to shop for a poodle.

The most important item I'd found in the bag was a wallet
with cash and a credit card in Brittany's name. It worked at the
luggage store in the Dallas/Fort Worth International terminal
where I found a shiny white leather carry-on bag. (I'd never
buy leather, but I figured Brittany would love its rich, supple
feel.)

The U.S. Fish and Wildlife Service could pull some strings
pretty quickly, it seemed. I hoped they were as good at wardrobe
assignments, because that's all I had to go on. Tan slacks and a
blue polo shirt. I was about to find out.

I flipped the straw hat onto my head, pulled it down, hoping
it would stay, and moved with the crowd toward the ground
transportation area, scanning for my new hubby. It felt like
a freak blind date, only I couldn't fake a migraine and slink
out the back door. I kept telling myself, no matter what, I was
going to smack him with a big kiss, right in front of everyone.
No one was going to accuse me of blowing an op.

As I approached the exit, I knew I was in Central America.
The cool of the air conditioning mixed with waves of humid,
tropical air and exhaust fumes wafting in from the street where

cars honked and engines ran, all maneuvering for the best spot.

I caught sight of someone waving. He wore tan slacks and a blue polo, but it couldn't be him. This man was young, tall and lean—one of those guys who crawls under razor wire and bounds over ten foot walls for exercise. I quickly scanned the luggage claim area for a balding man in the same get up. No one. I turned back. The guy was walking toward me, waving. I faked like I hadn't seen him the first time. "Hi Honey!" I called.

He walked toward me, his arms outstretched. I dropped my bag and lunged into his embrace. He lifted me up and spun me around. Wow, he was strong. I tilted my head back and he kissed me, long and hard. "I missed you," he crooned as he set me down.

Man, was he ripped, pecs firm as a ham hock. I lingered a moment with my hands on his chest, looking into his deep, brown eyes. He was my husband after all. I gave him my best Texas sweetheart smile. "I've missed you, too, darling." *Like, my whole life.*

Dalton gave me another peck on the lips, then, his eyes warning me to be careful, he nodded toward a man who hovered a few paces back. "George sent his driver. Wasn't that nice?"

I pulled away from his embrace and flashed my best Brittany smile at the man.

"He's invited us to dinner," Dalton added.

"Fantastic, I'm starving." I reached for my carry-on bag but Dalton grabbed it before I could.

"Let me get that," he said.

Maybe this marriage could work out after all.

CHAPTER 3

The drive from the airport was breathtaking in more ways than one. Costa Rica's countryside is lush with the dazzling greens of the rainforest and, as we got further west, occasional vistas overlooking the Pacific Ocean. It made me itch to go exploring. This tropical paradise has the highest density of biodiversity in the world. Nearly 500,000 species live here, hundreds of which exist nowhere else on Earth. With tropical rain forests, deciduous forests, Atlantic and Pacific coastline, cloud forests, and the coastal mangrove forests, the possibilities were endless for a nature lover like me.

The driving on the other hand was a free-for-all. Typical Latin America. Stop signs, yellow lines, no passing zones—all trivial suggestions only tourists take seriously, meaningless to the average tico, as the locals call themselves.

Dalton and I sat with his arm around me, snuggled up together, saying very little other than an ooh or ah at some vista and banal chitchat about the comfort of my flight and such.

At last, we arrived. George's palatial hacienda was tucked into the jungle a half-mile from the main road. Actually, it was more like a compound—three barns, a fenced horse pasture, surveillance cameras rigged at every corner.

Our car approached the main house, a sprawling ranch of typical Central American design—white stucco walls, red-tiled roof, expansive, open porch with a thatched overhang. The drive encircled a white marble fountain and led right up to the edge of the porch.

Four dogs, some kind of German Shepherd mix, came tearing around from the back of the house. Dogs will naturally guard a home, but their level of training speaks volumes about their effectiveness. The driver got out of the car and with a quick hand command, they retreated. Hm. Well-trained. The driver opened the back door of the car and offered me his hand to get out. One firearm in a shoulder holster, and one, I was sure, at his ankle.

I was ready to do my job, but honestly, I could have spent another hour snuggled up next to Dalton in the back seat.

I kept a grip on my handbag. My carry-on, in the trunk, would no doubt be ransacked while we ate. No problem. Nothing but clothes and my toothbrush in there.

George stood on the porch, his arms wide with welcome like Ricardo Montalbán in Fantasy Island. Now here's what I pictured. Old man with a potbelly, yellow teeth, and the dark leathery skin of one who's lived in the tropics for years. He'd combed his hair from one side of his round head, up and all the way over the top in an attempt to cover a shiny bald spot.

I tried not to stare as we crossed the porch. The white sport coat was just too much. He took my hand in his with a smile that beamed with delusions of being a rich and attractive playboy. All financed by exploiting animals. I hated him instantly. "Nice to meet you," I said.

"You must be thirsty, my friends. What can I get you to drink?" He turned toward a wooden cabinet stocked with bottles and glasses.

Dalton didn't miss a beat. "Scotch, if you've got it."

"And for the lady?"

"Oh, my. It's been a long day." I put my hand on my tummy. "I'd better eat first."

"Suit yourself," he said and splashed some Scotch into a glass for himself.

I stepped to the edge of the porch and scanned the grounds. One of the barns must have been where George housed the legal species. Snakes and frogs and such. Must have been where Dalton came to make buys.

Another car came up the drive, black, nondescript. It rolled to a stop and waited for the butler to emerge and call off the dogs before a tall, grey-haired man in his late fifties got out. Apparently, we weren't the only guests for the evening. George's driver got behind the wheel and drove the car away.

"Ah, Felix," George waved him in. "He's from Germany," he said with no further introduction. He dropped a few ice cubes into a glass, filled it with gin and a splash of tonic, then handed it to the man as he stepped onto the porch. So they were already well acquainted.

I moved next to Dalton and slipped my hand in the crook of his elbow, shyly hiding behind him the way a Brittany would do. Dalton introduced himself, then me. He obviously didn't know the man. Interesting. He didn't look like a henchman. He looked like someone's opa in a wrinkled polyester suit. His eyeglasses were made some time circa 1964, thick lens, greasy around the edges. Probably another buyer. When he shook my hand, I noticed a nasty gash notched in the fleshy webbing at the base of his thumb. Snake bite.

We settled into rattan chairs facing the fountain. I smiled. Felix smiled. Dalton took a swig of his Scotch.

The sun was setting fast, I noticed, and the drum of the rainforest insects increased, filling the awkward void. Soon, I heard the rumble of another car coming up the drive. Again, the dogs came running and were called off. A stocky man in his late fifties (early sixties?) got out, smoothed his white shirt, and took a cigar from the pocket. He took his time puffing to get it lit before crossing to the porch and barging in like a bull through the gate. "Where's my drink?"

It was Joe Nash. I was sure of it.

"Carl, you old bastard. You know Maria hates cigars in the

house," George said with a chuckle.

"I'll eat out here with the dogs, then," he said with a grin, took another puff.

"Carl, is it?" Dalton was on his feet, shoving his hand out. "John Fuller. Nice to meet you."

Nash nodded, his eyes immediately on me, looking me up and down. "And who do have we here?"

"My wife, Brittany." Dalton gave me a pat on the butt, nudging me toward Nash.

I suppressed my impulse to twist his arm off at the shoulder socket. Somehow I managed a grin and stepped forward to shake hands with Joe Nash, the legend. And called him Carl. Surreal.

George handed him a drink. Bourbon maybe. "Pura vida, mi amigo," Nash muttered, the cigar twitching with each syllable.

Carl, Carl, Carl. I drilled his name into my brain. The rich collector. So all three guests were buyers.

Headlights shined through the trees—another car coming up the drive. This time a hunky, cowboy-looking guy got out and sauntered our way. Introductions were made. Kevin, from Australia. Around thirty. Deep, husky voice. Easy on the eyes. Nice fitting jeans, white T-shirt. His wavy hair was cut short with a tiny curl at the back of his neck. He started talking about the weather, the ride over, how beautiful the rainforest was. My mind drifted in the direction of adultery, my fingers gripping that curl. Something about that Australian accent.

It seemed he was the last of those expected. The men made small talk, the boring small talk of those who aren't sure why they're together. They sipped their drinks, Nash absent-mindedly chewing on the cigar, until finally the butler arrived with news that dinner was to be served.

"Shall we?" George gestured toward the entrance to the main living area and the dining room, I presumed. The guests filed in. Joe—I mean Carl!—stepped to the edge of the porch, clipped the burning end off his cigar, and stuffed the chewed end back into his mouth. He gave me a wink.

The house had an open layout with white marble floors and oversized leather furniture. Ceiling fans slowly circled overhead. As we moved toward the dining table, a door opened and closed down a corridor toward the back of the house and two toy spaniels with oversized ears scampered toward us— clickety, clickety, click. "Ah, my wife Maria and her—" George glanced down at the dogs and curled his lip "—entourage. Frick and Frack."

Maria glided into the room, steady and comfortable on four-inch heels. Gobs of jewelry dangled from her neck, wrists, and ears. A beauty, and at least fifteen years George's junior, she was definitely a native tica. Wavy dark hair and creamy skin. George didn't make an effort to formally introduce her, so I knelt to pet the dogs.

"Look at those ears," I said. "They're so cute."

"Papillons," George muttered as he gestured for us to be seated.

"French for butterfly," I said as I rose.

He didn't respond so I turned to Maria. "The ears, like a butterfly."

She gave me a blank look. Perhaps she didn't speak English? Without thinking, I said, "Mariposas—" Then it hit me. It would be an advantage if they didn't know I spoke Spanish. (Or German for that matter. Or French.) Too late. Or was it? I looked right at Maria. "Did I pronounce that correctly?"

Maria smiled at me. "Sí, mariposas."

I shrank into a timid shrug. "I thought it would be fun to learn some Spanish while I'm here."

She gave me an amused grin and said nothing. She turned to her other guests.

We were seated around a table the size of my apartment. The place settings were bone china and real silverware. Our first course, a plate of cheeses and fresh fruit—mangoes, red bananas, starfruit—was already placed before us. The butler popped a cork on a bottle of Sauvignon Blanc. I recognized the label. "Excellent choice," I said to George. "You have impeccable taste." Doesn't hurt to butter him up.

The butler circled the table filling our wine glasses, the ladies' first, then back for the men. Dalton declined. Both elbows on the table, he shoved a hunk of cheese in his mouth. I thought to myself, would a Brittany scold him for his table manners? Probably not. I smiled at him. "You really should try this, honey. It's Kim Crawford." I handed my glass to him. His face was frozen in a blank stare. He grabbed it by the rim, like a beer glass, took a gulp, and swallowed. Cretin.

Kevin, the conversationalist, piped up. "What's so special about Kim Crawford?"

"Indeed," said George, his eyebrows raised. "What's so special about her?" His question sounded like a challenge. He flashed his toothy smile. Felix and Kevin gazed my way. The butler paused, waiting to hear what I had to say. I could feel Dalton tense up next to me.

I hate Barbies crashed into my thoughts. And I'm charming, dammit. Except when I'm not. Like when I try too hard to be charming. I wasn't raised in some rich family with uppity parents and nannies with British accents who taught you the proper fork to use or how to properly compliment your host. I've seen the world, though, just not from a Lear jet. My dad and I lived out of a backpack. I slept in a hammock. I had no idea there was such a thing as silk sheets. (And, man, would I love a set.) But wealth and prestige wasn't the only way to know wine. It was about sheer passion. And I have a passion for wine. If Poppy loves wine, then Brittany loves wine.

"Not her," I said to George. "Him. He's a winemaker from New Zealand's Marlborough region. He's known worldwide for this very wine." I turned to Kevin the Australian. "From down near your neck of the woods."

"Yeah, those Kiwis sure know how to squeeze a grape." He winked and took a swig.

"So do you own a pet store in Australia?" I asked, trying to direct attention from me.

Kevin glanced at George and shook his head. He crammed a piece of mango into his mouth.

"How about you, Felix? What brings you to Costa Rica?"

"Business," he said as though he were oblivious to any expected social nuance.

Okay. Shutting up now.

"Brittany," George said. "May I call you Brittany?"

I nodded.

He gestured toward my wine glass. "Please, tell me more about this vintage."

He's testing me, like Mr. Martin said he would. Am I really the rich Texas wife? The tiniest thing can give you away. Well, it ain't Barbies but here goes... I swirled the golden liquid around in the glass, then tucked my nose into the glass to take a sniff and savor the bouquet. I drew in a long sip, slurping so it would aerate on my tongue. Then I swallowed. "Bold fruit with a hint of melon. Finishes with a crisp acidity." I set the glass down. George was grinning. "My compliments," I said. "With its unique herbaceous flavor profile, it pairs quite well with the mango."

I thought Dalton was going to swallow his tongue.

George let loose a bellowing chuckle. "John, that's quite a lady you've got there."

Dalton grinned. "Don't I know it." He squeezed me to him and kissed me on the temple.

The kitchen door swung open and the chef came in pushing a rolling cart, atop which sat a silver domed platter. He wheeled the cart up next to George and with the sweeping gesture of a magician, lifted the lid, revealing a giant slab of prime rib, floating in its own bloody juices.

My stomach flipped. The thing is, I don't eat meat. Ever. Mr.

Martin's words rang in my head. *Keep your cover. Roll with it. Crap! What do I do?* I was prepared to kiss an old man. To play the rich, trophy wife. To carry a leather bag even. But I cannot, will not, swallow a piece of meat. *Oh my god, I'm going to blow this op right now. And I just got here.*

The chef sawed away at the hunk of flesh, cutting it into slabs a size no man should consume in one sitting. Of course, being the visiting lady, I was served first. The thing lay limp on the plate in front of me, visions of my eighth grade biology class banging in my head. Thirty-two thirteen-year-olds dissecting a cow lung. For some twisted reason, the others thought it was great fun to saw off spongy pieces and fling them at each other, to see if they'd stick. I promptly barfed on Sonny Davis' shoes, then spent the rest of the afternoon in the nurse's office, searching for a new career goal as my dream of being a veterinarian had vanished in one hands-on lesson.

I tried to vanquish the thoughts as I politely waited for everyone else to be served. I searched for ways to bow out. A coughing fit? Sudden case of indigestion? A phone call? How could I get the cell phone to ring right now? This moment was always awkward for me. *Thanks, but I'm a vegetarian. What? Are you crazy? Just try it, you'll love it.* People never got it. There was no way I could bring it up here, now. It would raise too much suspicion. Brittany was from Texas. A genuine beef-fed American.

Dalton had his fork in one hand, his knife in the other, sawing off another bite as he chewed an oversized hunk he'd already shoved in.

You have to do this, I told myself.

I got a piece on my fork, forced myself to open my mouth, shoved it in and clamped my mouth shut before I could change my mind. George hovered over his plate and gnawed off a piece, the juices dripping down his chin. He used a white cloth napkin to slop up his face. I was inspired. I picked up my napkin and, in a swift move I'd perfected as a child, as I wiped, I spit the meat into the napkin, then eased it into my lap. *Tah dah!* I only had to do that about twenty-seven more times without attracting attention.

Like angels descended from Heaven, two little butterfly-faced pups appeared, drooling on my shoes. My saviors. I slipped one bite to the floor at a time where it disappeared instantly.

Dalton must've sensed something was up. "Sweetheart, how are you doing? That's an awfully large portion."

"It's absolutely delicious," I grinned and took a gulp of wine, a fine Tempranillo the butler had poured while I had been distracted. "But I am getting full."

He stabbed it with his fork and dragged it to his plate, leaving a few drips on the table. I drew in a breath. "Honey, you're making a mess." I used my napkin to wipe it up.

He gave me the don't-embarrass-me-woman look.

I smiled and shut up, secretly thanking him.

At least I was now left to enjoy the rice and beans.

The conversation lulled while everyone chewed. Not that it had been a robust sharing of ideas before the meat arrived.

"So, Brittany," George managed to say through a full mouth. "I saw you looking at the horse barn when you arrived."

I halted mid-chew. "Yes?"

"Do you have an interest in horses?"

Horses. Not illegal, not a typical black-market species. My brain synapses fired away, crackling in my skull, searching for the right answer as I slowly chewed what was in my mouth before answering.

"Would you like to go horseback riding?" He glanced at Maria. "Perhaps you ladies could go tomorrow while John and I discuss business."

"Well, I—"

Dalton interrupted. "Brittany isn't really a horse person." Why was he saying this? Shouldn't I take any opportunity to connect, even if it was with the wife?

"Oh, I'm sure she'll love it." George turned to Maria, the first he'd spoken to her since we sat down at the table. "Le llevara a caballo mañana?" *Will you take her horseback riding tomorrow?*

She shook her head. "Tal vez en unos días," she said with a forced smile. *Perhaps in a few days.*

George turned to Dalton with an authoritative nod. "We'll make it work."

I finished my rice and beans in silence, my intuition buzzing. Something wasn't right. Something wasn't right at all.

CHAPTER 4

After a cordial drive through town, George's driver dropped us at our room—some rent-by-the-week kind of place. Individual thatched-roof bungalows dotted the property amid typical tropical landscaping, complete with roped walkways.

As we got out of the car, we were greeted by the on-site manager. He took my bag and led us to bungalow number eight. My spidey-sense tingled. This guy was too eager to help.

His uniform was a crisp white shirt with a tie striped in bold, tropical colors. His dark hair, cut into a terribly executed mullet, resembled a long mane and I instantly pictured Yipes, the zebra mascot for Fruit Stripe gum. (Yipes was my greatest hero for about four months when I was six because he donated five cents from each pack sold to the World Wildlife fund for the preservation of endangered species.) I had a feeling this Yipes wasn't such a good guy. He was probably being paid to spy on us. I'd have to keep my eye on him.

Dalton had his key in the lock and I got the feeling Yipes intended to follow us right in. I gave him a wink and told him to leave the bag. For good measure, I grabbed Dalton by the hand and swung him around for another kiss. After all, we were to make a good show, right? Like a good undercover agent, he went with it. He slid his hand around my back and pulled me up against him. "Feeling feisty, are you?" he said, his voice husky, his eyes drinking me in.

I wrapped my arms around his neck and we held there a moment, looking into each other's eyes with a playful tease. He leaned in to kiss me, then just as our lips met, he pulled back. *What are you waiting for.* His hands slid down from my back to my ass and with a gentle pull, I was pressed against him and the hard bulge in his pants. A warm heat rushed through me. He pushed the door open with his foot, kicked my bag inside, then pulled me with him as he backed into the room. I had the feeling he wanted to consummate this marriage post haste. Good thing Yipes had turn and fled.

As soon as the door shut, I heard, "So, you're Special Agent Poppy McVie?" I spun around. Special Agent Joe Nash stood there with his arms crossed.

"Yes, sir." I straightened my blouse, feeling as though I'd been caught kissing behind the school bleachers. "Reporting for duty, sir." I glanced around the room. "How did you…"

He nodded to Dalton. "I swept for bugs."

Dalton plopped down in the only chair in the room. "Nash, look at her. She can't be two months out of training." He gritted his teeth. "I told you this was a bad idea. This is too risky."

Joe held up his hand. "Now hold on—"

"You were there." Dalton got up from the chair, one hand gesturing in my direction. "She can't keep her mouth shut." His gaze swung around at me. His hands dropped to his hips. "My god, girl. What the hell was all that? I mean, who uses the word herbaceous? When you run off at the mouth, making stuff up, that's how people get killed."

I let him fizzle a moment. Calmly, I said, "First of all, I'm not a girl. Second, Martin told me to keep my cover as close to the real me as possible." I gave him a moment to ask. He didn't. "I was a sommelier in college."

Dalton shook his head and rubbed his eyes. "Well, you didn't have to make me look like an idiot. We're supposed to be married. You know, act like we like each other. It needs to be realistic, believable."

Nash grinned.

Dalton glared at him. "What's so funny?"

"Oh, trust me, it's believable."

Dalton threw up his hands. "I'm supposed to be able to trust her with my life." He glanced my way. "Do you even have any tactical training?" He looked back to Nash, but pointed at me again, his finger inches from my face. "I bet she can't even—"

I hooked my hand under his thumb, clamped down on his elbow with the other, and in one swift move, I twisted, collapsing him to the floor. I shoved my knee in his back. "Can't even what?" Holding him in the thumb lock, I leaned down and whispered in his ear, "Make you believe I'm actually hot for you?"

"Jesus Christ. All right already. You got something to prove. I get it."

"You should never let your guard down."

"What the hell? I shouldn't have to be on my guard with you. That's the point."

I looked over at Nash. He was shaking his head. I released Dalton.

"Strix recommended her," said Nash. "I trust his judgment. Deal with it." He gave me a stern look. "Work this out."

Dalton plopped back down in the chair. "Yes, sir."

Nash crossed his arms. "I don't need to be playing referee for God's sake. I shouldn't even be here. I wanted to make sure you were fully briefed and the two of you have a game plan. "

I sat down on the edge of the bed. "Sorry, sir. I do have some questions. Mr. Martin knew very little. He said you'd brief me."

Nash nodded. "About nine months ago, we nailed a smuggler in Miami with a primate. The intel from that bust led us to George. Our ultimate goal here is to identify the kingpin. For now, he's the target of our investigation, but we're not sure it's him. We think he'll lead us there." He grinned. "Tug on one hair and you'll find it's attached to the whole beast.

He went on. "I've been posing as a rich collector, having been referred by a friend, a guy we busted last year. George has been chummy, but not giving anything up yet. He's shifty. He mainly likes to drink and golf. Dalton's been working his way in as a wholesaler from the states. He makes regular buys, all legal species. He's been trying to take it to the next level. He can tell you about it. The point is, we know George is involved. All the connections lead to him. But he has a very sophisticated system of avoiding any direct communication. He doesn't make the offer to sell. He's too smart. He knows that's what we need to nail him. Dalton has been doing excellent work, though. We figure it's imminent."

"But so far you have no hard evidence?"

"This is Special Ops," said Dalton. "We don't gather evidence, we gather intelligence."

"What about the other agent, García?"

Nash shrugged. "He's working the poaching side alone, trying to identify the buncher. A buncher—"

"Is the middleman, I know. Buys from the poachers."

Nash nodded.

"García sent Martin a post card from a palapa bar down on the beach, The Toucan. On the back he scribbled a message: Having a great time. Have my sights set on a beautiful butterfly. Mean anything?"

Nash shook his head.

"Is this bar connected to George in any way?"

Nash shrugged. "Not that we know of."

I looked at Dalton. "Maybe we should check it out."

He shook his head. "No. Don't you get it? We can't stick our noses in on his op and risk being recognized. We stick to the plan. As soon as I get the call, you choose your monkey. Then you're on your way home."

"That's it?"

Nash held up his hand. "I need to get some shuteye." To Dalton he said, "You two need to get to know each other tonight.

Make sure she's prepared. Read her in on anything you've told George about the two of you, your life, your history." He smiled at me. "Welcome to the team. Let's nail these bastards."

"Thank you, sir." I rose. "One more question. Who are Felix and Kevin?"

"Never met them before. As far as I can tell, they're potential buyers as well."

"Why would George bring us all together for dinner? They seemed just as perplexed."

"Maybe he wants us to know there's demand," said Dalton. "So he can get a higher price."

Nash shrugged. "Another thing we need to figure out."

Dalton went to the porch door. He scanned the grounds before gesturing to Nash that it was safe to leave.

Just like that, we were alone.

I plopped my bag on the bed and sifted through it for my toothbrush. "So start from the beginning," I said. "How'd we meet?"

Dalton rubbed his eyes. "You came into one of my pet stores one day, looking for a cat, and it was love at first sight. Whirlwind romance, married two months later. That was three months ago. We live in Dallas, Texas. Our stores are called The Pet Corner, which is a real business by the way. The owner works with us." He took a business card from his wallet and handed it to me. "Here. Memorize this."

I scanned the card. "I've already—"

The bathroom door slammed shut.

Seriously? I plopped down on the bed. This was not going as I'd hoped. The shower started running.

I got up and opened the door and went in and sat down on the edge of the sink. His shirt and pants were neatly folded and stacked on a tiny table in the corner. "Why the attitude?"

He poked his head out from behind the curtain. "What the

hell, woman?"

I grinned. "It's alright. We're married."

He groaned. "Unbelievable." He yanked the curtain shut.

"What's with the monkey?"

Dalton didn't answer. All I could hear was lathering soap and splashing water.

"Strix said I was here to pick out my own monkey. Why wouldn't you just choose one? You're the buyer."

The water shut off and he reached out from behind the curtain for a towel. A moment later he slid back the shower curtain. He was standing there half naked, the towel wrapped around his waist, wet hair, water dripping down his chest. I swallowed. He was ripped. Not an ounce of fat.

He raised his arms to comb his fingers through his hair and I noticed the tattoo, the SEAL Trident.

"You were in the Navy."

He glanced at the tattoo and frowned.

"My mother was in the Navy. I recognize the symbol. You were a SEAL."

He turned toward the mirror, ignoring me.

"Unless you rang the bell."

He glared at me.

"No, of course you didn't."

He took a long breath as though contemplating whether he wanted to make me disappear without a trace. He was a SEAL; there was no question whether he could. My mother warned me against dating SEALs. They're crazy, she'd said. Every last one of them. No daughter of mine, blah, blah, blah. That's all I remember actually. But if Dalton was a SEAL, at least I knew something about him. Something significant. It takes a certain kind of man to be a SEAL. A man of honor, loyalty, and integrity, not to mention grit, tenacity, and discipline.

"White-faced Capuchin."

"What?" I snapped back from my thoughts. He was lathering his face with shaving cream.

"I was testing the waters, asking for a class II species, see how he'd react."

"And?"

With an old-fashioned straight razor, he shaved one side of his face, taking one swipe, then another before rinsing it.

"And he asked about the buyer." He scraped the razor under his chin and up to his lip, then rinsed it and started up the left side of his face. "See, you have to understand, these guys get nervous about new people in the pipeline. They don't like surprises." He splashed water on his face and used the hand towel to wipe it dry. "He was getting squirrelly."

"Squirrelly?"

He flipped up the toilet seat, waited. When I didn't move, he turned to me. "Do you mind?"

I crossed my arms.

He rolled his eyes and reached under his towel.

"Fine," I said and backed out of the bathroom, shutting the door behind me. I stared at the queen-sized bed. It had been awhile since I'd had a man in my room. Suddenly I was imagining him naked, the lights off, the—the door swung open and Dalton came out of the bathroom wearing the same pants, no shirt. He strode over to face me.

I swallowed hard, getting my head back on straight.

"I didn't want to lose the ground I'd gained. So—"

"So you said it was for your wife."

He thrust his jaw forward and nodded ever so slightly.

"And he suggested you bring her down here, implying she could pick it out herself." So that was it. Dalton screwed up. He had given George an open door to call his bluff.

He leaned forward, his face close to mine. "I don't need you to tell me how to do my job."

"I didn't say anything." I could feel his hot breath on my face. I tried to keep my voice non-confrontational. "Now here we are. In this whirlwind romance."

He held my gaze for a long moment. Then smirked.

"Yeah."

I broke away and went back to my suitcase. "What was all that about horseback riding with Maria?"

Dalton shrugged. "What do you mean?"

"It seemed like an opportunity to get close to George. Why wouldn't we do it?"

"You need to follow my lead, not question everything." Before I could respond, he screwed up his face, annoyed. "We just need to be cautious, that's all, not seem too eager. This is a delicate thing."

"All right," I said, staring at him. What was that all about?

"When the time is right," he said. "You can chat and do whatever it is women do."

"Whatever women do?" Wow, he was a piece of work. "And what was that outside the door a few minutes ago? Is that just what men do?"

He glanced at the door and I could read his thoughts. "I was playing a role."

"Really?" I said. "You weren't the slightest bit into it?"

His eyes lit with fire. "Hey honey, I'm a healthy, virile man. You were rubbing up against me."

Two could play this game. "Just playing my role, *hubby*." I crossed my arms. "Speaking of that, I don't get Maria. She doesn't seem like a woman who would go for someone like George. She was too—"

"You need to work on your observation skills. Didn't you notice his fat wallet? A lot of women find that pretty darn attractive."

"I know, it's just that—"

"That's what women do. Act all aloof and independent, suck you in, then whine when the dough dries up."

I shook my head. "You don't have a girlfriend, do you?"

He huffed. "Divorced."

"Shocking," I said. With those strong arms and his boyish grin, he oozed sex in an all-American kinda way. "I bet you were a football player and made all the cheerleaders swoon. She was the prom queen, right?"

"Listen, you're here for one thing. Until then, your job is to look pretty and keep your mouth shut. Go shopping, go to the beach. Get your hair done." He threw up his hands. "I don't care."

"Let me get this straight. I'm to do nothing, say nothing? Even think nothing?"

"Now you're getting the idea."

"You don't care about my experience, my abilities, my skills." I slammed my hands down on my hips. "I'm only here because I have boobs."

His eyes dropped to my chest. "And you've come with very fine assets." He ripped the cover from the bed, plopped down in the chair, and drew it over his head. "Goodnight, sweetheart."

CHAPTER 5

I took a cold shower. I still didn't sleep well. Too many things about this whole situation bothered me. Namely, Special Agent Dalton. What the hell? He practically had me panting for him and then claimed it was all an act. Asshole. My mother was right. What really bothered me was that I couldn't decide which was worse—him or my mother being right.

I rolled over but couldn't get the image out of my mind of him standing in the shower with the towel wrapped around his waist. I really needed to get out of the north woods. I loved the boreal forest, but the boyfriend prospects up there were nonexistent. I contemplated a second cold shower, forced my mind elsewhere.

Why had George brought all the potential buyers together for dinner at his house? What would be the advantage? If anything, you'd think a savvy business man would want to keep his associates from talking to each other. There had to be a logical reason.

And the postcard from García. He must have thought Nash could put it together. A beautiful butterfly. What in the world did he mean by that? Butterflies were big business on the black market. But he hadn't mentioned one species specifically? I needed some knowledge of local butterflies.

When dawn rolled around, Dalton grunted something about going to do his job, to have fun at the beach.

Like hell. I wasn't going to sit on my hands and do nothing. I was going to the palapa bar, see what I could find out. I know how to blend in, be discreet. Unfortunately, it wouldn't be open for several hours, so I had time for my morning yoga. After that, I decided to check out the butterfly garden. Worth a shot. Maybe I could get an idea of what García might have been referring to on the postcard.

I brushed my teeth, tied my hair back into a ponytail, threw on a t-shirt and shorts, grabbed Mrs. Strix's handbag, and headed out.

The valley surrounding our bungalow had a mix of tourists, ex-pats, and snowbirds. A nice walking path had been slashed through the edge of the jungle for ease to the shopping district where one could find all the modern conveniences yet still feel as though in a tropical paradise.

The morning air was cool. I took my time, enjoying it. This close to the equator, afternoons could be oppressively hot and muggy. I've never understood the phrase "tropical paradise." It's an oxymoron, if you ask me. Heat and I don't mix.

There was no denying though, this truly was a nature lover's paradise. The trees were filled with birds, squawking, chirping, chattering. An iguana scampered off the path where it had been basking in the morning sun.

From above, I heard a distinctive swish in the canopy. Two white-faced capuchin monkeys scampered across a limb like a couple of squirrels. The way these two could romp through the treetops was breathtaking to watch. They dropped down, one at a time, to swing on a hanging vine, then flip over onto the next limb, keeping balance with their prehensile tails. One seemed to notice I'd stopped. He sat back on his haunches, his arm around a branch, his round, black eyes lit with curiosity as he chittered at me with his high pitched call.

He reminded me of the Philippines and the tarsiers I loved as a kid, though the tarsier's ultrasonic call is inaudible to the human ear. With large, bug-like eyes and long, bony fingers, they grasp a branch in a pose that always makes them look like they're hugging it.

My dad would get me up before dawn and we'd hike into the forest, to a blind he'd placed the day or two before, and we'd wait for one to come along and then hope for the light to be just right for the perfect wildlife photo.

I wished I had a camera with me right now. The capuchin was so close and seemed unafraid in my presence. I lingered for a while, watching the two watch me. This is why I'm here, I thought. This is how it should be.

Before I moved on, I glanced behind me and caught sight of Yipes, several paces back, trying to act nonchalant. So I had a tail. Hm. Good to know.

I continued down the path toward town and found the butterfly garden tucked away on a side street, a tiny educational building serving as its entrance. I went inside and wandered for a few minutes, taking in the layout, before I was greeted by a guy about my age, an American with movie-star good looks. "Bienvenida al Jardín de Mariposas," he said in greeting.

I understood him perfectly, but I had to keep my cover. "Um…hello to you, too. Do you speak English?"

He gave me a smile that made me smile involuntarily in response. "Welcome to the butterfly gardens." His voice had husky, earthy notes, a sound that belonged in the bedroom. My bedroom.

"Oh, thank goodness," I said. I stared a moment too long.

He stood with his weight on one leg, his hand on his hip, exuding an easy confidence. He knew he was hot. His long hair was tied back in a ponytail at the base of his neck. His square jawline and scruffy stubble made me want to tug him into a dark back room and go crazy. *Damn Dalton for getting me all revved up.*

I shoved my hands into my pockets to hide the monster diamond on my left hand, thinking how ridiculous it was to have to hide my fake ring because of my fake husband that I wasn't getting any action from anyway, fake or otherwise.

"Would you like a tour?"

Um, with you? Yeah! I glanced down at my shoes. *Poppy, get it together. You're a federal agent for god's sake.* "Yes, I think so," I said with a shrug, trying to act indifferent. *Wait. Maybe this guy has some information. And flirting will get me a lot further, get him talking, won't it?* "When's the next one?"

"Oh, we aren't that busy. I can take you right now, if you'd like."

As I ransacked my purse for the ten dollar fee, I slipped the ring off and let it drop to the bottom.

"We're a non-profit, supported completely by donations and volunteers."

"You're a volunteer then?" I said, stating the obvious. *Geez. My hormones must be eating away at my brain cells.*

"A couple days a week."

I glanced around. "Are you the only one here?"

"Yeah, we're a pretty small operation."

"And what's your name?"

"Oh, I'm Noah. Glad to meet you. And you are?"

I stared at him, my mind blank. For the life of me, I couldn't come up with my cover name. "Noah, that's a nice name," I said, stalling. "I get it. As in the guy with the ark." His expression changed. *Oh my god. I'm such an idiot.* "Oh my gosh, I'm sorry. That's really your name, isn't it?"

He cocked his head to the side, a look of confusion on his face.

"I figured you must get a lot of children and"—*kill me now*—"that was part of your, you know..."

He gave me a genuine smile. "Naw, we don't get a lot of kids. Wish we did, actually."

I extended my hand. "Well, I'm Brittany. It's nice to meet you, Noah. "

"Likewise," he said, and led me to the insectarium, a room rimmed with glass aquariums, each housing some exotic native insect—beetles of all sizes and shapes, scarabs with iridescent green shells, spiders that would make my mom vow to never set foot in this country. Posters adorned the walls showing comparable sizes of insects, butterflies, and moths, as well as paintings from local artists, and a large case of pinned insects.

Noah patiently told me about each live insect—its lifespan, eating habits, predators—while taking it from its tiny habitat and holding it out for me to see. "Half of the species on Earth are arthropods," he said.

"That's a lot of bugs. I'm glad they're not all as big as that one." He was holding the Hercules Beetle, a bug the size of an Idaho potato with horns. He assured me it was harmless and offered to let me hold it. He looked surprised when I took it and held it in the palm of my hand.

He grinned. "Wow, most ladies won't touch him."

I looked right into his eyes. "Well, I'm not like most ladies."

His eyes turned sultry. "I can see that."

We moved out of the building to the gardens, several of which were designed to replicate different natural habitats from low-elevation forest to cloud forest, a habitat rare on Earth save for a few specific locations, one being right here in Costa Rica. Each was enclosed with netting to keep the butterflies in.

In the first, I learned about the Blue Morpho butterfly, the pride of Costa Rica. One lighted on his hand and I swear its wings spanned eight inches. When it opened its wings, it shined a brilliant iridescent blue, but the underside of the wings was a dull brown color with swirls and eyespots. Noah told me that in flight, the contrasting bright blue and dull brown colors flash, making it appear as though the butterfly is magically appearing and disappearing, inspiring countless tales in local folklore.

As we moved on through the other gardens, Noah told me about the unique glass-winged butterflies that don't rely on bright coloring, but rather use pheromones to attract a mate. I could have told him a thing or two about the effect of pheromones right now.

The last stop was a giant leafcutter ant colony. Noah seemed to come alive as he spoke about it. Next to humans, he said, leafcutter ants form the largest and most complex animal societies on Earth. Deep within their nests, the ants work collectively to cultivate a fungus that grows on their chewed leaves—gardening to produce their own food.

Through observation, scientists realized that certain species of leaves, avoided by the ants, tend to possess compounds called terpenoids, a breakthrough discovery of antifungal chemicals now used for medicinal purposes or fungicides.

Noah relayed this information to me as though it were the most amazing discovery of mankind.

The tour ended back in the tiny building in which we had started. Noah gestured toward the items for sale in the room—artwork, jewelry, books, nature guides. "All the proceeds from our gift shop support our conservation efforts and the upkeep of the gardens here, the care of the butterflies, that kind of thing." He pointed to a jar near the cash register. "And if you can, we're asking for donations for our capital campaign to build a wildlife sanctuary here for animals that have been injured or orphaned. Our goal is $200,000."

Normally, I'd empty the bottom of my handbag of all its loose change for such a thing, but I couldn't risk my cover.

I stood there, trying to search my rational mind for insight. Could Noah be involved somehow with the smuggling? After all, I'd come to the butterfly garden to poke around, see if there was any connection to the clue from Agent García's postcard. It certainly would be an excellent cover. No one would suspect. I glanced at Noah. No way.

I chose a book, *The Birds of Costa Rica*, and paid cash. "Do you know of any good birding trails?" I asked.

He gave me a free map of the area and pointed out a few of his favorite spots. I thanked him, stuffed the map in my purse, and lingered. I didn't want to go. He had some kind of gravitational pull.

He leaned on the counter. "What brings you to Costa Rica, anyway?"

I smiled. I could stay and talk with him all day. Maybe he'd take me by the hand and lead me into that back room. "The birds, actually. I'm kind of a bird nut. I was hoping to see a keel-billed toucan. And the resplendent quetzal, of course."

He nodded. He understood my obsession. "I know a tree cavity where I've seen a family of toucans. You interested?"

My eyes lit up. "Yeah!" I yanked the map back out of my purse and opened it on the counter. "Where?"

"I'm done here in an hour. I could show you." His eyes had that hungry-for-me look. My breath caught in my throat.

"Well, I, uh." Darn, I had work to do. "I really have to get back right now. But, maybe later?"

He nodded, looking disappointed. "Sure."

My gaze lingered on his lips. "No, I'd really like that," I stammered. "I'll stop back by." I scooted out the door before I could spontaneously combust.

For my next stop I needed to be sure to ditch Yipes. He wasn't that difficult to spot, but I had to be careful. There are two tried-and-true ways to lose a tail: the covert maneuver or the distraction. Yipes seemed like the type who'd fall for a good old-fashioned distraction. I walked back to the bungalows and knocked on his door.

"Buenos días, Señora Fuller," he said. "How may I help you?"

"Would you please call a taxi for me and point me in the direction of a drug store. I need, well, some woman things."

His cheeks burned and he nodded. "Uno momento." He slipped back into his room. That ought to do it.

I had the cab drop me at the drug store in town where I picked up a new beach bag, yellow flip-flops, and some cheap sunglasses, then went around the block, rented a moped for the week, and headed for the beach.

Most people would be thrilled to spend the afternoon sipping pineapple drinks on a sunny tropical stretch of sand. I am not most people. I hate the sun. Or I should say, the sun hates me. Red hair, freckles, pasty white skin. While my high school girlfriends strived for the tanned little bunny look, I worked hard to avoid the crispy lobster imitation.

The Toucan palapa bar was more my style. Its giant thatched roof was nestled among the palms, providing glorious shade. Brightly-colored, hand-painted signs directed beach-goers down a roped path toward shrimp skewers and ice cold margaritas. (Obviously for tourists who have no knowledge or interest in true local fare.)

I tucked my hair under the hat, donned the sunglasses, and strolled in.

The place was packed. Jimmy Buffet blared from speakers mounted at every corner. Waitresses bustled about delivering metal pails filled with Cerveza Imperials. The mixed scents of stale cigarettes and spilled beer hung in the open air.

Every inch of wood in the place—supporting posts, table tops, chairs—had names and dates crudely engraved, testaments to memorable drunkenfests. At the bar, a group of six college kids simultaneously tipped a bamboo log with shot glasses attached while their friends pounded on the bar, making memories of their own.

I sidled up to the bar and elbowed in. A young tica with her hair pulled back in braids hollered, "What can I getcha?" as she hustled by, her arms loaded with fried fish baskets. Her name tag read Isabella.

"Do you have a local IPA?"

She dropped the baskets in front of the bamboo shot meisters, grabbed a bottle from the cooler, and popped the top as she headed back toward me. "Eight dollars," she said, but kept walking. I pulled out a ten and before I could drop it on the counter she was back, plucked it out of my hand, and was off again.

"This place always this busy?" I asked the guy holding down the bar stool next to me.

He leaned over. "Cruise ship lunch rush." His lip curled up on the left side in an attempt at a grin, his blood alcohol content apparently causing partial facial paralysis.

I looked in the direction he was making a valiant attempt to point. The shipping dock jutted out into the ocean directly to the south of the bar where a large white vessel with bright orange lifeboats was docked.

I ordered some gallo pinto, Costa Rican style rice and beans. I was going to be here awhile.

At the other corner of the bar, a couple college boys posed for a picture holding a six-foot boa constrictor. One of their drunk pals held out a twenty to take his turn to look macho holding a snake that was probably nearly comatose.

A sign hanging behind the bar read: Animal photos, $20 - Birds, snakes, monkeys. Above the sign, two scarlet macaws perched in the rafters. Scarlet macaws are highly intelligent, and with their bright red, yellow and blue plumage, they make popular pets. For that reason, they're endangered in most of their habitat, making them a CITES class I species. One bird can sell for thousands of dollars on the black market. Someone in possession really should have a permit, but in Central America, keeping animals like these is culturally ingrained and rarely prosecuted. The Costa Rican government concerns itself primarily with illegal export. At this point, these two birds couldn't go back to the wild anyway. They'd probably been in this bar their entire lives.

I sipped the beer, killing time, watching the staff. This seemed like an unlikely place for a wildlife poaching connection. A lot of money was being passed over the bar, though. I watched one of the bus boys put every third bill into his front shorts pocket. Interesting, though not my concern. I was keeping an eye out for anyone named Paco. Maybe I'd get a glimpse of my fellow agent.

Every once in awhile, a man came from the back, went straight to the cash register, took out some cash, then went back out. Some buying of something was going on out back.

After about an hour, most of the patrons staggered toward the boat gripping plastic souvenir cups in the shape of pineapples in their sweaty hands. The music was turned down and I could actually hear the surf as it rolled on the beach. The bartender came back by. "Another IPA?

"Sure, why not?" I dug out another ten spot.

A young couple lingered at the end of the bar. Newlyweds. The girl pointed at the rafters. I glanced in the direction she was looking. A white-faced capuchin swung from a rope. The girl giggled and nodded and her pink-cheeked husband tossed a twenty on the bar. The monkey swooped down with a screech, snatched up the bill, and raced back to his perch. The newlyweds frowned. "Hey," the husband called.

Isabella whistled and gestured to the monkey. He skittered and chirped, then reluctantly descended to the bar. The wife opened her arms and the monkey curled up in her embrace. He cowered, his eyes darting from her to her husband. How could no one see how terrified he was? She cooed at him like he was a baby.

I had to admit, he was cute with his round, black eyes set in that adorable little human-like face. That's what made them highly sought after for pets. Unfortunately, it's often people like this, animal lovers, who do the most harm. They don't stop to think; these are wild animals. Sure, they look like cute little babies when they're young, their faces and hands so much like ours, but once they hit puberty, they can be aggressive. Wild animals are meant to stay in the wild, not interact with people. If I wasn't undercover, I'd be over there explaining all that to them right now.

Isabella kept a close watch on the monkey. She knew. The

husband snapped a few pictures, no doubt for their honeymoon Facebook page. That's when I noticed the monkey's right hand was missing. Poor thing. Often, monkeys are caught in primitive snares which can do all kinds of damage as the monkey freaks out trying to get free. Most likely that's what had happened to this little guy.

The monkey loped across the bar where Isabella provided a treat, then he scampered back up to his ropes. So sad. "How long as he been here?" I asked her.

"Clyde? Oh, dis one a few years." She ran a wet rag down the length of the bar. "De owner has had many, all named Clyde. You know, from de Clint Eastwood movie."

"That was an orangutan," I said.

With an eye roll, she said, "I know." She headed for the beer cooler, but made an abrupt turn, headed back toward me and quickly started restocking the plastic cups. A tico in his fifties, his dark hair slicked back, entered the bar area carrying a black satchel. He reminded me of an old, washed up Hispanic version of Vinnie Babarino.

"Who's that?" I asked.

She kept her head down. "Oh, dat Carlos. He de owner."

Carlos grabbed handfuls of bills from the cash register and stuffed them into the satchel. He called Isabella over to him. Her shoulders turned inward and, with her eyes downcast, she obeyed. He whispered something to her and glanced around the bar. I turned to the side and tipped up my beer so he couldn't see my face. Then he was gone.

Isabella returned to the bar. "Another?" she asked.

I shook my head. "He looked familiar. I think he's a friend of my brother. What's his last name?"

She glanced his way as though she wanted to be sure he was gone. "Mendoza."

"No, not him," I said. "Oh well." I shrugged. "How long have you worked here?"

"Too long," she said and moved away. I finished my beer, set the empty bottle on the bar, and gave her a wave. That's all I was going to get for today.

I took a walk down the beach and punched up Mom on my cell phone. It rang five times before Mr. Strix picked up. "Everything okay?"

"Yeah. I was hoping you could look someone up for me."

"I'll do my best."

"Carlos Mendoza. He owns The Toucan, the bar on the postcard."

"How'd you get his name?"

"Long story. Could you also scare up a picture of García?"

There was a pause. "I'll see what I can do. Hey, Roy called. He said to tell you they nailed the guy."

I smiled. "And Honey Bear?"

"Roaming free."

I smiled wider.

"So, Mendoza. How'd you—"

"Sorry. Gotta go." I hit end and headed back toward the bungalow. I didn't want to have to explain.

Within ten minutes, I got a text with a photo. It could have been the man who'd gone to the cash register, but I wasn't sure. Mr. Strix called back. "You're not going to believe this. The Mendoza family is quite large. Most live in Nicaragua. Besides the bar, a few years back, the family purchased a coffee plantation in Costa Rica. It's no longer producing, but get this: it borders George's property."

Bingo.

CHAPTER 6

If Carlos was the buncher, he needed a remote location to house the illegal animals, keep them fed, alive. It needed to be far from the eyes of the law or meddling neighbors. Like an old coffee plantation.

After a quick exploration with Google Earth, I had a pretty good sense of the lay of the land. Only one structure still stood on the property, one that looked large enough to house animals—the old roasting shed. That had to be it. But I needed to find out for sure.

Field trip!

The farm sprawled across a steep hillside, quite rugged terrain compared to some of the larger plantations, leaving few locations for coffee trees. The rest appeared to be wild jungle. A river ran through the property from the northeast, meandered through the east quarter, then exited its boundary just north of the southeast corner.

The driveway, a rutted two-track, would likely be under surveillance. The best place to enter the property unnoticed was at that southeast corner, south of the river. It was going to be a trek.

I strapped my binoculars on my chest, tossed my new bird book in my backpack, laced up my boots, and was out the door. What better disguise than a bird nut, hopelessly lost in search of the resplendent quetzal?

From the edge of the dirt road where I stashed my moped among the tangle of jungle, I followed a power line for about five hundred yards, then headed up the side of the hill. I was in pretty good shape, but the humidity was stifling. My T-shirt was soaked in minutes. Flashes of color flitted through the trees—motmots and trogons, parrots and toucanets—birds I'd loved to have the time to stop and identify.

I did keep a sharp lookout for snakes, though. Central America is not a place to underestimate when it comes to poisonous creatures, especially the slithering kind. I didn't want to stumble across a fer-de-lance. There was a reason it was known as the ultimate pit viper. Most snakes will avoid contact. When threatened, the fer-de-lance rears up and advances. The darn thing can strike above the knee cap. It produces an overabundance of deadly venom and isn't afraid to use it. Forty-six percent of snakebites in Costa Rica come from this guy and they aren't pretty. Symptoms rival that of simultaneously stepping on a land mine and being sprayed with poison gas. Yeah, I was watching my step.

I turned twenty-five degrees and walked another four hundred yards figuring I'd arrive just south of the shed. When I got to within one hundred yards, I stopped dead. Good thing I'd been watching so diligently for snakes. About six inches above the ground ran a primitive tripwire—a thin cable stretched horizontally through eye hooks that had been drilled at the base of trees, then upward to an iron bell that hung about twenty feet in the air. Clever. Simple, yet effective. I stepped over it and crept forward more cautiously. Someone was definitely guarding something.

I found a perch in a banyon tree with a decent view of the shed. On the southwest corner, a guard paced back and forth in a way that was clear his training came from watching Schwarzenegger movies. Not good. He could be unpredictable, therefore dangerous. He carried an old rifle of some sort, its barrel wrapped with electrical tape.

The sturdy old structure he guarded was tucked into the hillside, longways. Corrugated tin walls supported a split-style roof that provided a three-foot gap at the peak for air circulation and natural light. Large bay doors stood open on either end, east and west. The driveway came up from the east.

On the open, flat land south of the shed, large, flat concrete slabs had at one time been used to spread coffee beans to dry in the sun. Beyond that was jungle. Two more guards with similar technique to the first paced at the edge of the clearing.

Using my binoculars, I scanned the eaves of the shed. No video cameras. In fact, looked like there was no electricity. I thought I heard the faint hum of a generator. Perhaps for lights at night?

I slipped back into the cover of the jungle and, keeping to the harsh, late afternoon shadows, I headed up the hillside on the west side, avoiding the driveway, to get a look from the north. I came across three more trip lines, the same setup, each attached to an old bell.

About five hundred yards from the northwest corner of the shed, I crossed a path that disappeared into the dense foliage. I followed it to a ravine where a cable stretched across from which a metal basket hung, large enough to carry two people. It was rigged with a pulley system that allowed the basket to be moved by hand in either direction. On the far side, all I could see was an outhouse. I hadn't noticed it on Google Earth, but it was small and tucked under a tree. It would be too risky to get in the basket to check it out. If someone came along, I'd have nowhere to hide and nowhere to go. Besides, it might squeak and rattle and bang. I slipped back among the leaves and headed toward the shed.

I stayed on the north side, uphill of the shed, and crossed all the way to the east to a vantage point where I could clearly see the main entrance. Two guards posted there carried 9mm submachine guns, looked like MP-5s. There was definitely something of value in there. I crouched down on my haunches and wondered how I was going to get inside to find out.

And how I was going to tell Dalton.

I had to assume that if the place was guarded, it was guarded twenty-four hours a day. I could set up a diversion to draw the guards away, but, working alone, that would likely provide very little time to get inside and back out. I could do a stake out, see what comes and goes. But that kind of operation took more time than I had and required constant surveillance, which I couldn't do alone, nor could I make excuses for the time away from Dalton. Bribing one of the guards for information was way too risky; I could blow my cover.

I decided to pack it in. This was all I was going to get today. I circled back around to the south side of the shed and dropped into the thick brush when a bell rang somewhere to the west of me. *Crap.* I looked down. I hadn't tripped a line. I was sure the closest one was a good twenty paces to my left.

Shouts came from the shed. The guards were scrambling. I had to get out of here. And fast.

A second bell rang. This time closer. Someone was coming my way and closing in fast. If I ran, I'd be spotted. I dropped to the ground and rolled under some ferns. A man went barreling by, laughing as he went. I pushed up on my elbows to get a glimpse of him. He went straight for the next tripwire, jumped up and down on it, causing the bell to clank back and forth. When he turned to listen for the guards, I got a good look at him.

It was Noah. I blinked. From the butterfly gardens. What the hell was he doing?

He took off, heading south, then dropped with a thump. He let out a moan.

Crap. I couldn't afford to get caught here. But I couldn't let him get shot.

I scanned the jungle for pursuers, then left my hiding spot and sprinted to him. He was rubbing his right shoulder. "Is it broken?" I whispered.

"No." He got up and brushed mud from his shorts. It took a moment, but I could see recognition set it. "What are you doing here?"

There was movement behind him. I held up my hand in a gesture to be quiet. He turned to look and I slipped behind a tree. A guard burst through the brush and skidded to a halt, aiming his weapon at Noah. "Ah, ha! Te he cogido," the guard muttered. He turned his head and drew in a breath to shout. I pounced, slamming him to the ground. I knocked the rifle from his hands and with a quick punch square on the temple, put him out cold.

"Holy crap! Where'd you learn that?" Noah said, his eyebrows arched all the way to his hairline.

"Self defense class?" I shrugged, trying to look surprised myself. "Ha, who knew it would pay off?" I grinned.

"Yeah," he said, staring at the guy.

"I think there might be more coming," I told him. *Four to be exact. Two heavily armed.*

"Yeah." He turned east. "Follow me."

I hesitated. I had no idea what Noah was up to or why he was here.

"C'mon, trust me," he said and flashed his adorable smile. "You don't want to stick around."

I glanced down at the guard. At this point, my fate was tied to Noah's anyway. He launched into a full-out sprint, crashing through the brush. I followed as he ran down a shallow ravine, up and over a ridge. Shots rang out behind us and a bullet went zipping by my head. And Noah was headed toward the river. We needed to cut south.

"I think there's a river ahead," I said. "It's whitewater. Too strong to cross."

"I know," he said and kept running.

"But—"

"Trust me," he hollered over his shoulder.

The land sloped downward and we burst through some thick

foliage at the edge of the river. "Go, go, go!" Noah shouted as he plowed into the water. I glanced around. In a small eddy just downriver, a young woman sat in a two-man inflatable kayak, a paddle in one hand, a rope loosely tied around a tree trunk in the other. She let loose the line and dug in with the paddle, shoving off. "C'mon," he shouted to me as he launched himself into the kayak. I hit the water and in two strides I was straddling the edge of the kayak, one leg in, one dragging, as it caught in the main current and sent us spinning.

He grabbed me under my arms and heaved me up and into the kayak. "Hang on," he said. "Whatever you do, stay in the boat. Listen to Claudia. She's a world-class rafting guide."

Water gushed and roared as it propelled us downriver in a turbulent, angry fury of white foam. I glanced back at Claudia. She looked calm and capable, focused on calculating the flow of the rapids. "Sounds goo—" I managed to say before we rammed a wall of water and white froth crashed over my head. I gripped the sides of the narrow boat with both hands and blew water out of my nose.

Noah dug in with his paddle at Claudia's commands. "Forward, now back paddle," she hollered over the thunder of the rapids as we spun sideways and rolled up one side of a crest and down the other. "Duck!" Our boat scraped under branches that jutted out from the bank. "Now hard left!" Noah obeyed and no sooner were we facing downriver than we hit a rock and the front of the kayak shot upward, stalling on the rock, jolting us to a halt as water roared past.

The back end slowly caught in the current and spun us around, lifting us off the rock, shooting us downriver facing backward, bobbing in the waves. Claudia looked over her shoulder. "Get ready," she said. Ready for what, I wondered, and we were airborne. Claudia dropped down, clinging to the back side of the kayak, as it flipped. Noah launched into the air. I rolled into the churning maelstrom, my arms flailing, grasping in the air for anything. Then the boat was there and I grabbed hold and heaved myself up onto it, coughing water from my lungs.

"Where's Noah?" His head popped up to our right, then got sucked under again.

"Grab him!" she shouted.

I reached out and when he popped up again, I grabbed ahold of his T-shirt and hauled him onto the overturned kayak. He coughed and sputtered.

Claudia managed to get us into a backwater at the edge of the river and we got the kayak flipped back over. "It's not over yet," she said.

Noah and I got back into the boat. Claudia gave it a shove into the current and crawled onto the back. The kayak bucked and tilted as we hit some big swells, then just as Claudia got her paddle in the water, we slid into a white hole of swirling water. The kayak jerked and spun in a white vortex, water pounding over us from all directions, pummeling us with surge after surge while Claudia shouted commands to Noah. I felt helpless, hanging on to the sides. Finally, the bow tipped upward and we shot out of the hole.

The kayak rolled sideways, then with a jolt, rolled the other way as Claudia shouted, "Lean left! Now right!" We countered our weight and managed to keep it upright as we squeaked through a narrow gully, water smashing into boulders on either side of us. "Hold on!" Claudia warned. The nose dipped downward and we plunged over a waterfall. Wham! We rammed into the water, slamming us forward. We hit the water so hard my eyelids yanked wide open and my eyeballs were washed inside and out. I let go to give them a rub and the kayak dipped and spun sideways, tipping to starboard. Somehow, Claudia kept us upright.

Then finally, the kayak slowed in a stretch of riffles. Noah got up on his knees, held the paddle over his head, and shouted, "Ha! Take that, you bastards!"

Claudia paddled us around another bend to where the river crossed under the road and they'd stashed a beat up old VW bus. We hauled out, strapped the kayak to the roof, and after three attempts to get the engine started, sped away, Claudia at the wheel and me and Noah on the floor in the back.

As soon as we caught our breath, Noah asked, "What were you doing up there?"

"I was out birding and kinda got turned around, I guess." I conjured some surprise and added a helping of fear. "Then you ran by and scared the crap out of me. Who were those men? They were shooting at you! At us!" *And why were you purposefully ringing the bells to get them to chase you?*

Claudia glanced back at Noah and something passed between them.

"I guess I'm lucky you came along," I said.

"I'm pretty sure it's the other way around." He shook his head. "Claudia, you should have seen her take down that guard."

I winced, but he didn't notice. That was an unfortunate complication and could be a problem. "He's making it sound like more than it was," I said, trying to produce a blush. "He scared me is all. I just reacted."

"Sounds like he got what he deserved."

Noah gave her a quick shake of his head. He looked at me and grinned.

If they were organized activists, they'd be cautious. Too many questions right away would cause suspicion. But I had a thousand. What did they know exactly? How had they found out about the shed? Did they know who was involved? I had to be careful. I wouldn't force him to give me an explanation. Better to act the flirt, see how things played out.

"All I know is we stumbled onto something." But I didn't want to look like an idiot. With narrowed eyes, I looked to Claudia and back to Noah. "Wait a minute. Are you cops or something?"

"Ha," he huffed. He shifted his weight and leaned forward. "Do we look like cops?"

I smiled and shook my head. He was looking mighty scrumptious with wet hair and his damp T-shirt clinging to his chest. If Claudia was his girlfriend, I needed to be extra cautious. I think he read my mind because he said, "You're shivering." He held out his hands, gesturing for me to scoot over and lean against him. "C'mere." I flipped around and cuddled into his embrace. "You should come to the bonfire tonight, meet the gang. Claudia's boyfriend will be there and Jack's doing a fish boil."

I grinned. "I'd like that." *And all the intel you can give me.*

CHAPTER 7

I wondered how the agency governed undercover affairs, what was allowed, how one handled *relationships*. I fully understood the risk in becoming emotionally involved, but a little fun while getting information couldn't hurt, could it? The agency had no authority over my sex life anyway. Maybe some fraternization clause, but civilians were none of their business. Besides, I needed to work this informant for all I could, right?

All this flashed through my mind when Claudia hopped out of the van, leaving me alone with Noah, his warm breath on my neck. He ran his hands up and down my arms. "We should get you out of those wet clothes," he whispered in my ear, his voice husky. My breath caught in my throat and all I could manage was to nod.

The back doors of the van flung open. "Looks like Jack's already got the fire going," Claudia said.

"We'll be out there in a minute," Noah said as we piled out of the van.

The sun hung low on the horizon. The surf rolled on the beach, its lapping mixed with the happy sounds of friends gathered near the crackling bonfire.

Noah took me by the hand and led me down a narrow sandy path, swatting palm leaves out of the way. He came to a halt at a clearing and spread his arms wide. "My humble abode," he said. Nestled in the branches of a tree was a tree house. An actual tree house. Okay, it was partially supported by poles, but it was the coolest house I'd ever seen.

Tiny solar powered lanterns lit a spiral staircase leading up to the rail of the balcony where a hammock hung.

"Nice digs," I said.

"Be my guest." Noah gestured for me to climb the stairs.

As I reached the top, my mouth dropped open at the view. I leaned on the railing and took it in. An amber glow lined the horizon. Pink clouds streaked across the sky. The bonfire below us sent rosy sparks into the air, soaring skyward.

Noah came up behind me and wrapped his arms around my waist. "You like?"

"It's beautiful," I said, steadying myself.

He nuzzled my neck. I held my breath.

He pressed his lips to my ear. "Your heart's racing."

"Yeah, I just, you know, I'm just a little on edge. It's not everyday I get shot at."

"I know." He flashed a conspiratorial smile. "Isn't it invigorating?"

He gently turned me around to face him. One hand on my hip, he reached up and caressed my cheek, then slipped his hand behind my neck. He paused, inches away, his hungry eyes lingering on my lips. I ran my hand up his arm, across his shoulder to his neck and pulled him toward me. Our lips met. His tongue touched mine and made my insides twinkle.

"Mmmm, I like your style," he said with a grin and kissed me again. His hand slid down from the small of my back, sending warm pulses up my spine. I twirled the hair at the base of his neck in my fingers, gently tugging. He pulled me closer and nuzzled my ear, then my neck. His stubble rubbed against my flesh and made me shiver.

"Where's the beer?" someone called from below. I backed into the rail. Noah held me, his strong hands keeping me pressed against him.

"The cooler's by the shed," he said. "Should be full."

"Right on, bro," the voice called back.

I pulled away from his embrace. This was getting too hot, too fast. I had to keep my head straight. "I should get changed," I said.

He hesitated as though trying to read my thoughts. "Sure." He padded across the wood plank floor and soon candles lit the room with a soft glow. To one side, comfy rattan chairs, a coffee table, and a bookshelf stuffed with paperbacks made a cozy living room area. At the edge of the railing stood a bar with two barstools. On the other side, drawers and a wardrobe were built into a solid wall, to the right of that was a wooden door. Beyond, a roped bridge led into the darkness, to another tree house possibly. A ladder reached upward to a tiny loft where I could see the edge of a queen-size mattress. The ceiling was part thatch roof, part plastic sheeting. A single fan slowly turned overhead.

He took a T-shirt from a drawer and handed it to me. "Bathroom's there," he said and pointed to the wooden door.

"Thanks." I couldn't get away fast enough. I splashed cold water on my face. What the hell was I thinking? I quickly changed into the T-shirt, stuffed mine in my backpack, looked in the tiny mirror, and took a deep breath. *Keep your act together, McVie.*

I shot a text off to Dalton: Will be late. Don't worry.

"Much better," I said as I emerged from the bathroom and sashayed toward the staircase. I could smell something roasting on the fire. "I'm hungry."

"All right then," Noah said.

I felt a twinge of regret.

Noah's friend Jack had the fire stoked enough to run a steam engine. To the side, atop a huge pile of coals, a makeshift pot, some kind of sawed open half metal barrel, bubbled with boiling water. Jack tended a basket, pulling it out to check the contents, then dunking it in again, each time causing the water to run over, sending up a whoosh of steam. The gang (I counted eight friends plus Noah) was gathered around the fire, watching Jack's elaborate show. Each time he dunked the basket, they stepped backward for fear they'd singe eyebrows.

My throat started to tighten with the familiar anxiety. "What's for dinner?" I asked, trying to get myself prepared. I have this thing about mystery food.

"Wisconsin fish boil," Jack said. "Sans the fish, of course." He yanked the basket upward again, poked at a potato with a stick, and nodded with satisfaction.

He carried the basket to a picnic table that had been covered in newspaper and flipped it upside down. Potatoes, corn cobs, onions, and what looked like chunks of squash tumbled onto the surface. "Grub's up!"

Noah handed me a plate, then whistled. Everyone turned their attention to him. He pointed to me. "This is Brittany." He made a vague gesture and said, "The gang." I smiled. Some nodded, smiled. That was that. I was accepted. Either Noah was their indisputable leader or they were a pretty easy-going group.

I waited my turn to take a helping of the vegan fish boil, then as everyone settled into places around the fire, their plates balanced on their knees, bottles of Cerveza Imperial propped up in the sand, I tried my best to chitchat. Not my specialty. But I wanted to have a good sense of who these people were.

Claudia and her fiancé, Matt, guided rafting tours on the Grand Canyon in the summers and spent about three months a year in Costa Rica. "It's affordable and gorgeous. What more could a couple of river rats want?" Matt said.

Dan and Sierra guided kayakers in Alaska for four months, then helped run a zip-line tour here in the winter.

Doug was an actor/part-time bartender. "Between jobs," he grumbled.

Amanda and Colette were a lesbian couple who sold handcrafted jewelry in the summer art show circuit. Amanda did freelance computer work, so they would travel with an RV chock full of jewelry, then park it at her parents' place in Silver Springs, Florida to take two months off in Costa Rica every year.

Jack cleaned windows on skyscrapers in New York City and made enough cash to hang the rest of the year "surfin' the CR, livin' the pura vida."

"What's your story?" Jack asked, then promptly shoved an entire red potato into his mouth.

"I'm kinda between semesters," I said. "Trying to find my way, you know."

This brought a lot of sympathetic nodding around the fire.

From the darkness, a monkey came scampering across the sand, leaped onto the table, grabbed a potato, and ran off, chittering with glee, the potato tucked under his arm like he'd been trained by the Green Bay Packers offensive coach.

"Clyde!" someone yelled.

"Hey Isabella," Noah called. Coming up the path was the waitress from the palapa bar. *Crap.* What was she doing here? What was their connection?

"Hola de nuevo," she said and went right for a plate. Clyde followed on her heels. She plopped down, cross-legged in the sand next to the fire and stabbed an onion with her fork. Clyde cowered behind her. Apparently he wasn't fond of fire.

"C'mon." Sierra slapped her thighs and Clyde leaped into her lap. She stroked his head and he cuddled against her.

Isabella swallowed her onion and looked at Claudia. "Did you get anything?"

Claudia glanced at me and shook her head.

Isabella looked at me and in a moment, recognition showed in her eyes. I had a choice. Claim a coincidence and hope they weren't too skeptical, or hit the thing head on, making them believe I'm one of them. Easy enough, but I had to have an explanation for being at the shed. A good one. Now.

"You must be wondering why I'm here. Hell, I'm wondering why I am here." I turned to Noah. "I wasn't birding today." I clenched my teeth together in a please-don't-be-mad-at me grin. "I was snooping. I think something illegal is going on up at that coffee shed." I turned to Isabella. "And I think your boss has something to do with it."

Next to me, Noah set down his fork. "What do you mean?"

"Well, I *was* out birding, a few weeks ago, and I saw these men. They had a bunch of animals in cages. Not chickens, but monkeys and other birds." I shook my head. "That's not right. So, I know it was a fool-hardy thing to do but—" I shrugged "—I found out who owns the property and that he also owns The Toucan. I'm not sure what I thought I was going to do when I found out the truth. I just couldn't stand to see animals being hurt like that, you know." I leaned forward and raised my eyebrows to show how scared I'd been. "I wasn't expecting to get shot at!"

It was subtle, but I could see nods around the group. They were accepting me. Noah finally said, "You're right. Something is going on. Those men are poachers. The worse kind. They capture live animals, snatch 'em right out of the forest, enslave 'em and sell 'em like plastic toys."

"No way," I said. "I knew it. That's awful." *Interesting.*

"It's big money. Right under our eyes, wildlife is being plundered and sold on the black market."

"How do you know all this? You said you aren't cops."

"No. We actually make a difference."

"So you're like some animal justice vigilantes?"

He laughed. "Yeah, something like that."

I smiled at him with eyes that said, *that's sexy,* which it was. "Cool."

That was it. I was part of the gang.

Isabella turned back to Claudia. "So how'd it go?"

"We're going to need a better camera. It's just too dark in there." She frowned at Noah. "I'm sorry. You did a great job distracting them. I had plenty of time."

So that's what they'd been up to. In the U.S., it's not uncommon for activists to try to expose cruelty and wrongdoing via videotaping. PETA has been quite successful with that approach, bringing some lawsuits or government action against the perpetrators. But in those instances, animals were being held legally. The video tapes revealed cruelty and abuse. Carlos's activity was obviously illegal, so I wondered what exactly this group was planning and what they thought they'd accomplish.

I nibbled on my cob of corn, trying to act interested, but not too much in the details.

"We'll get the footage," said Noah. "We just need to be patient."

"We should storm the place, set 'em all free, and burn it to the ground," said Matt, the river guide.

"Yea-ah!" said Jack. "Bring it on, baby!"

Colette shook her head. "It's a holocaust that's never going to stop."

"They sell a product like any other business," said Noah. "It's all about the money. We hit 'em in the pocketbook and they'll take notice."

"Yeah, but how do we do that?" Amanda put her arm around her girlfriend. "Meanwhile, innocent lives are at stake."

"I know. I know," Noah said. "We've talked about this. To beat them, we have to think like them. Find their weakness. Wildlife trafficking is big business, but it's got to be volatile."

Claudia piped up. "You mean supply and demand. But every time we set some animals free, they just go back into the forest and trap more. Demand is the problem."

They nodded in shared frustration. Claudia frowned. Amanda hugged Colette tighter. Jack and Matt took chugs of their beers. I feared the conversation was fizzling. "So why the video?" I asked.

"Sun Tzu," Noah said with a grin. "Know thy enemy."

"So you're surveilling the buncher, trying to find a way to

destroy his business, that it?" I said.

Noah looked at me and smiled. "That's the plan."

"But what might you learn from the video?"

"Schedules. When they have inventory of what. To sustain a business with live inventory, they must be hedging somehow, probably selling futures, but that involves its own kind of risk. If they can't deliver, they'll lose their clients."

Interesting approach. I wanted to ask more about it, but it didn't feel quite right to push any more than I already had right now. One thing was sure, Noah wasn't a typical activist. He had significant intel and would be a valuable asset. There was more to him than I had first thought.

"We could use someone like you on the team," he said with a wink as he rose to his feet and brushed sand from his shorts. "Hey, throw me another beer," he said to Doug, the actor, who was at the table getting seconds.

Sierra spoke up. "As long as you agree, wildlife belongs in the wild."

I secretly thanked her. She had given me another opening to drive home that I'm one of them. "You say that, but what about Clyde?"

Isabella answered. "He can no go back now. He never survive."

"But isn't he your pet?"

"No me." She seemed insulted. "Carlos. He don care nothing bout him. I take care him."

"Oh, sorry. I didn't mean anything."

"You should meet him." She gave Clyde a hand command and he leaped off Sierra's lap and scampered over to me. "Go ahead, pick him up."

I reached down and picked him up like a toddler. He snuggled into my lap. I couldn't help myself. He was adorable. I scratched his ears and, he snuggled closer. Cute little bugger.

Noah grinned at me. "Clyde's kinda our mascot. He's one of the gang." He chuckled. "He's even helped with the cause."

Balled up napkins started flying Noah's way. One walloped him on the side of the head.

"What's this about?" I asked.

Noah pointed at Jack. "See, Jack had this brilliant idea—"

"Hey, it was brilliant. It worked."

"Right," he said through a chuckle. "He rigged up Clyde with a GoPro camera, strapped it right to his chest."

"Monkey-cam!" roared Jack.

"Hear, hear," shouted Doug, raising his beer.

"Hear, hear," everyone responded and tipped their bottles.

"We were up there at dawn. Clyde was all fired up. We'd been working with him on drills, commands, you name it."

Clyde stirred in my lap. He knew they were talking about him. He buried his head under his arms.

"Hey, you're embarrassing him," said Dan.

Noah continued. "They only had one guard at the time. He was sound asleep. We sent Clyde in."

"So, what, Clyde was supposed to walk through the barn with the camera running?" I asked.

"That was the plan." Noah threw his head back and roared with laughter.

Jack plopped down in the sand, resigned. "The little shit. He ran straight to the first cage with a female, flipped the latch, and went at her like a dog in heat."

"Yeah, chicka-baum-baum," said Doug, grinding his hips. "Making his own monkey porno." He put out his hand, palm up. "Gimme five."

Clyde pounced from my lap, climbed up Doug's leg, and slapped him on the hand.

"Sure, you've got that mastered," Jack said.

Matt nudged Jack. "Hey, a guy's got his needs, man."

Claudia elbowed him in the gut. "Exactly. We should have sent a girl monkey."

"Hear, hear," said Colette, raising her bottle of beer.

"Hear, hear," chanted everyone.

More beers were passed around. Claudia got up and headed for the tree house.

I told Noah I needed to use the bathroom and followed her. A little girl talk was in order.

When she came out of the bathroom, I plowed forward, head on. "I really like Noah." I managed a blush. It was true. "What's his story, anyway?"

"We all love him. Great guy, but—" Claudia shrugged "—he's a bit of a mystery. Trust funder maybe." She grinned. "He's single though. But one thing I know for sure, you'll need a bull whip and a prod to tame that boy."

When I got back down to the fire, Noah had a guitar balanced on his knee and he was entertaining the group with a Woody Guthrie tune. A joint was passed around. I faked a drag. Noah covered Bob Dylan, Joni Mitchell, and even some John Denver while the others lazily sang along.

Soon, couples started retreating into the darkness and Noah and I were left alone at the fire.

"I like your friends," I said. *If only the circumstances were different.* "I feel comfortable here."

"Yeah, they're a good bunch."

"How'd you meet them?"

"Oh, you know. We share interests."

I wanted to know more about them, about him, about the smugglers, but I couldn't figure out a way to ask right now without being obvious. I stared into the smoldering coals.

"You're welcome to stay," he said. "I promise to keep my hands to myself."

"Now, why would I want you to do that?" I crawled toward him across the sand and hit him with a kiss that made his toes curl.

"Mmm, exactly," he moaned.

I pulled back. "But I really have to go." My mom always said, leave 'em wanting.

I caught a taxi, found my moped where I'd left it, and hurried back to the resort.

I didn't want to wake Dalton, so I slid the door open and quietly stepped into the dark. A flashlight beam blasted me in the face. My hand flew up to cover my eyes. "What the hell?"

"What the hell is right? Where have you been?"

"Following a lead."

"A lead? A lead!" Dalton flicked on the lamp and stood with his arms crossed. "What did I tell you?"

"Didn't you get my text? I did what you told me. I went to the butterfly gardens. Absolutely amazing what they're doing over there, by the way. You should stop in. They have an insectarium and four gardens, each dedicated to—"

"What's your point?"

"A guy who works there knows about the smuggling operation and—"

"What? Seriouisly, Poppy. It just happened to come up in conversation?" He nodded, mocking me.

"Well, yeah, one thing led to another, and the next thing you know, I'm invited to a bonfire with him and his friends. I found out that—"

He held up his right hand for me to stop and rubbed his forehead with his left. "I don't want to hear it."

"But—"

"I don't care what some civilian renegades think they might know."

"But they've seen things. They have evi—"

The hand went back up in my face. "I have been here for nine months. Nine months working this case." His eyes crinkled with worry and frustration. "Do you have no respect for what I've worked so hard to build here?"

"Of course I do. But you weren't there."

He turned away from me and lowered himself into the chair. "Stay away from them."

"Listen to me," I said. "The information they have, I know

it's valid."

"Oh, and how do you know?"

I hesitated. I couldn't tell him I'd been there. "I just do. I trust them—"

"Are you listening to yourself?" He got back up from the chair and got in my face. "Trust them? They're civilians. There's a reason we don't include civilians in our operations." His eyes were on fire. "You're going to blow everything."

"That's not fair. Just because you don't know me yet—"

"Don't you understand? This isn't a game, little *Poppy*."

I crossed my arms. "How dare you?"

"You're gonna get us killed." He threw up his hands and plopped back down into the chair.

"You don't trust me."

His eyes snapped to me. "Damn right I don't trust you! I don't know you. As far as I can see so far, you're a serious liability." He lay back in the chair. "I don't care if Joe likes you. One more stunt like that and I'll send you packing."

"Yes, sir," I said and turned on my heel and headed for the bathroom. I brushed my teeth, taking my frustration out on my gums, and when I came back out, Dalton was stretched across the bed. The blanket was piled on the chair.

CHAPTER 8

Dalton tried to slink out without a word.

"Wait, where are you going?"

"I'm going for coffee."

"Aren't you going to have breakfast with me?" I asked. Maybe I could get him to listen to me this morning. "We don't want them to think we're fighting."

"Why not? We are fighting. Spouses fight."

"Fine."

"Fine."

As soon as he shut the door, I threw the pillow across the room. *Dammit!* I had risked getting caught, ruining my career, blowing this op, everything, to get that information, and all for nothing. He wasn't going to listen to me. I stomped around the room, threw a few more pillows and kicked the bed before I slumped into the chair. *Dammit!*

A few minutes later he was back with two cups of coffee. He handed me one. "Get ready. I want to stroll around the shopping district, look like tourists," he said. "I could use a new pair of sunglasses anyway."

Shopping? Really? What would we learn there? I had to admit, though, it did seem the logical thing that John and Brittany would do. I grabbed my hideous handbag and we headed for town.

The old-town shopping district was a hodgepodge of tiny

stalls where local craftsmen hocked their handcrafted wares. I preferred it over the glitz of shoe, handbag, and perfume counters. This was a group of real people with real lives, trying to make a living for their real families. Not some faceless corporation from a foreign land.

Brightly colored sarongs and dresses livened the spaces with reds, yellows, and greens. There were hand tied hammocks and straw hats, wood bowls, cutting boards, trinket boxes, and hair pins made from exotic native woods.

We wandered through, looking for nothing in particular, Dalton holding my hand. It was hard to stay mad at him while he was holding my hand. I bet some marriage counselor had figured that out.

As I came around a corner, I spotted Yipes in the crowd. I spun around, wrapped my arms around Dalton's neck, and gave him a big kiss. "We have a tail," I whispered.

"Ah, you noticed," he said with a grin, his eyes on me.

"It's Yipes, the guy from our bungalow."

"Yeah, he's been—" He drew back and looked at me with a baffled expression. "Yipes?"

I started to open my mouth.

"Forget it," he said. "I don't need to know." He ran his fingers through my hair and pulled me toward him for another kiss. Dammit. Why'd he have to be so yummy? Jerk. This Jekyll and Hyde thing was going to put me into a tailspin.

"We should split up. You keep shopping, keep him busy. I'll meet you back at the bungalow for dinner."

I nodded and watched him walk away.

I exited the other side of the shopping area into a fruit market. Boxes of ripe bananas, mangos, watermelons, and coconuts were stacked on plastic crates. I selected a banana and paid. An Afro-Caribbean beat pulsed through the streets. I wandered toward the performers, then stopped and looked around. Head slap. Dalton had ditched me.

Fine. Two could play that game. I would take advantage

of the time to get better prepared, make sure I was ready for anything. Mrs. Strix had hooked me up with some realistic girly items, but she'd never been an agent. I needed a hardware store.

Around the corner and down the street, I found what I needed. A Leatherman tool, matches, lighter, heavy-duty string, tiny mirror, mini-mag flashlight, and assorted other items. I thought about a hand-held recorder, but like a gun, if I got searched, it could get me killed.

Now that that was done, what to do? I started toward the butterfly gardens then stopped. I needed to be careful. Dalton had been right about one thing, I had been reckless. Noah set me on fire. I could get burned. But oh my god, that kiss. A warm sensation came over me thinking about it. What's wrong with working an informant? Male agents do it all the time.

I sat down on the curb. Dalton made me want to scream. Noah made me want to scream, but in a different way. My head was mush. I went back into the store, grabbed a pre-paid phone card, then found a pay phone around the corner and punched in the country code and the number. After three rings, he answered. "Yo."

"Chris, it's Poppy."

"Girl, what's going on?" Chris is the only guy who gets to call me girl. We've known each other since sixth grade in the Philippines. When we ran into each other again in high school, half way across the world, we figured we were destined to be friends for life. Now he's a flight attendant for Delta airlines and I see him every few months or so, depending on how many layovers he spends with his latest flame.

I hesitated. I shouldn't have been calling him while undercover.

"Wow, silence. Something must really be wrong. Talk to me."

"I'm all right. Just frustrated. I wanted to hear your voice is all."

"Honey, what have I been telling you? You've gotta get out of redneckville and get properly laid. Come with me next weekend. I'm on a five-day Shanghai right now, then I've got four off. We could pop down to the Caymans. Drink some margaritas, watch those tight-assed college boys play beach volleyball. What do you think?"

"I can't. I'm in—" *Crap.* "I can't get away right now." I sighed. "I've been reassigned."

"What do you mean, reassigned? Poppy-girl, that doesn't sound good?" He paused a beat. "What'd you do?"

"Nothing! I busted the Lawson boys. But this is…Listen, I can't tell you. I just wanted to say hey."

"Well, now you've got me worried."

"Well don't. I can handle the job. It's just—"

He drew in a quick breath. "Oh my holy-hell. It's a man."

I blushed. Only Chris could make me blush. "It's complicated."

"Oh my holy-hell, it's two men. I just talked to you last week. You were bellyaching about rednecks and lumberjacks and now you got a love triangle going on?" I heard the rustle of blankets and his hand over the phone. It was the middle of the night in Shanghai.

"I'm sorry. I didn't realize what time zone you were in."

"No, no, no. I picked up, didn't I? Now tell me everything. I want every juicy detail. Like what are you doing in Costa Rica?"

Crap. Double crap.

"You think I don't know the country code? It's on my caller ID. Hey, are you on the Pacific side? There's a great hotel with a swim up bar that—"

"No, some bungalow in the valley, Arenal Gardens or something, and—never mind, I can't talk about it." I glanced down the street, one way, then the other. A random pay phone wouldn't be tapped, but being on it might cause suspicion. "You know, sometimes my work, I can't talk."

"Um, sweetheart, you called me."

"I know."

"This is much more than guy trouble, isn't it?"

"I'm sorry, love. I gotta go." I hung up. *Crap. What was I thinking?* He'd understand; I'd explain it all to him at Christmas. But that was a dumbass thing to do. I gritted my teeth. *That was a rookie move, McVie.* If I didn't watch my step, Dalton would boot me before I could stop my head from spinning. I needed to be more careful.

I circled back through the hardware store. I'd forgotten electrical tape. *Definitely not on my game. I need to step it up.*

I found a little cafe serving Costa Rican fare that had several vegetarian options. I sipped an iced tea and went over what had happened so far in my mind. Mr. Strix had told me to follow protocol, to listen to my SAC. But Dalton was so damn aggravating. My mother always accused me of having issues with authority. Damn, I hated when she was right.

After I finished my meal, I decided to take a walk, look for birds, at least I could add a few to my life list while I was here, when my phone rang. It was Dalton. "Where are you?"

"Why, I'm shopping, darling. Where else would I be?"

"Get back to the bungalow. I got the call."

Hot damn! Lights, camera, action. I'm going to pick a monkey.

The call came as an email. Anonymously, of course. We were to be ready at the bungalow for a white panel van to pick us up at seven o'clock.

"Are you ready for this?" Dalton asked.

"Bring it on. Let's do this thing."

"You understand, the van is so we can't see where we're going. They'll want us disoriented. And we'll likely be in an isolated location. We're on our own. It could get ugly. "

"I can handle it."

He paced.

I said, "Somehow I don't think a Navy SEAL would get so nervous about a simple covert action."

He glared at me. "I don't like wild cards."

I shrugged. "I'm your loving wife, wanting a pet monkey. Nothing more. Nothing less. It's simple."

He grimaced. "Why do I get the feeling nothing's simple with you."

Seven o'clock rolled around. No van. At seven-twenty-two, a white, solid sided panel van rolled into the parking lot. The back door opened and Dalton and I hopped in. One man drove while another man in the back motioned for us to sit on the floor and stay there. There was no confusion about it. The men were both native Costa Ricans, nothing particularly notable about them. They were delivery men. That was all.

We made a right out of the parking lot, drove about two miles, then made a left, then an immediate right, then we were in a roundabout. *Crap.* Or a parking lot, though driving in circles might bring unwanted attention. The van circled several times. Difficult to keep north from south, but I kept my head down. I was sure we straightened out again heading in the same direction we'd started—north.

After seven minutes of driving, two lefts and a right, we slowed and turned onto a gravel road or driveway. The van bumped and rocked over potholes for about two miles, then turned left again, this time immediately heading uphill, crawling along on what must have been the driveway. We were getting close and I had a pretty good idea where we were.

The van came to a stop. They made us wait inside for something, then the back doors creaked open and we got out.

It was dark, but there was no doubt—we were at the Mendoza family coffee plantation. I recognized the shed. *I was right. I knew it—oh crap!* I dropped my head and stared at the ground.

What if the guard I clobbered is here? What if he recognizes me?

A man approached from the shadows. "Bienvenida," he said. It was Carlos. I smiled and tried to act excited. "This way please." As soon as he turned, I scanned for others. If that guard was here tonight, I was screwed.

There was no breeze. Musty smells hung in the stagnant humid night air. As we approached the dark shed—Carlos, me, then Dalton—the animals started to stir and make noise. "So you have those cute monkeys with the white fur face, right?" I said, trying to sound like the snooty Texan wife I was there to play. "I don't want one with a black face, looking like he's dirty all the time." Carlos stepped inside the shed, flipped a switch, and the tired fluorescent bulbs flickered to life.

I stopped mid stride.

Cages were stacked wall to wall, the stink unbearable. Flies buzzed everywhere. The cages near the top were stuffed with birds—yellow-crowned parrots and keel-billed toucans. One toucan squawked and fluttered, banging its huge bill against the walls of the cage, feathers flying everywhere, its raw flesh exposed, ninety-percent of its feathers gone. A lump formed in the back of my throat.

Another cage was full of tiny chicks. Stolen right from their nest. I clenched my teeth together.

Below that were the monkeys. Some shook the doors to their cramped cages, their cries high-pitched shrieks. Others cowered in the corners. One pulled at its fur, patches of red skin exposed where it had yanked out handfuls. My stomach churned, bubbling up angry acid at the back of my throat. *Calm down. Take a breath.*

A three-toed sloth lay on top of one of the crates, hog-tied, his little arms pulled behind his back. My own voice screamed inside my head. *How can you be so cruel?*

One of Carlos's men took a stick and rapped on the cages, hollering for the monkeys to shut up. If one let out a shriek, he'd poke it through the bars, jabbing at the sorrowful creature.

For a moment, I lost all sense of orientation. I was sure I'd descended into the depths of hell. How could this be happening? Why? I reached for Dalton to steady myself.

Carlos was oblivious. He went straight to a cage which held a tiny white-faced capuchin, opened the door, and grabbed it by the scruff of the neck. "Like this one?" he said and held it up. It squirmed in his grip, its tiny, round eyes lit with terror. "This one's a female," he said. Her fur was matted and caked with grime. He held her out for me to take. The lump in my throat grew larger. I reached for the monkey and faltered. My throat started to constrict. *No, no, no. Poppy, keep it together.* I took the monkey in my hands and the poor thing shook with fear. "No, this one's no good," I managed to say.

Carlos shrugged, took the monkey from me, shoved her back in the cage, and slammed the door shut. He moved to another one, reached in and grabbed this one by the tail, dragging it out as it screamed. I couldn't breathe. No air. Not enough air. "He's a feisty one, but he already knows some tricks," he said and shoved the monkey at me. It grabbed hold of my hair and tried to climb over my shoulder. Dalton snatched it from me and handed it back. "Too active," he said. With his steady hand on my shoulder, I drew in a breath.

Carlos nodded. He went for a third one. "I've got just the right one for you," he said. He reached into a lower cage and tugged out a baby capuchin, still docile and trusting. He held it out for me to examine, its body cradled in one hand while he had ahold of it by the neck with the other, the way a sommelier would display a bottle of wine for the buyer to read the label. A baby girl. Her little arms flailed, her tiny, human-like hands reaching for something to grip.

By the grace of some patron saint of undercover agents, I managed a smile and took the baby monkey in my arms. She looked up at me with wide eyes, her little nose twitching. Her tail curled around my wrist. I thought of Clyde, how he had snuggled against me just last night, how he too had been taken from the wild, snatched from his mother, robbed of his beautiful, natural life. I swallowed, trying to be rid of the lump in my throat.

This baby monkey mewed, a high-pitched whistle, calling for its mother. A tingling sensation pressed behind my eyes. *Tears coming. No, no!* I blinked, trying to hold them back. Blood thrummed in my veins and my lip began to quiver. My breath started to expose me. I sucked in air and shook as it rumbled into my lungs. I turned to Dalton. "Oh, John," I managed before the dam broke open and tears streamed down my face in a warm, blinding flood. I snuffled and brayed and snot came out of my nose. "I'm so sorry about the baby," I cried. "If we hadn't lost the baby."

He put his arms around me. "It'll be all right, my darling," he said. "I'm sorry, guys. My wife, she's had a tough time of it." He rubbed my back. "I thought she was ready, but, you know."

"Yeah, whatever," said Carlos. He took the capuchin from me. "Let's go."

We were led right back to the van and it was over. My one job to do here and I failed miserably. I couldn't handle it. *All those animals... I leaned into Dalton and let him hold me all the way back to the bungalow.*

I went straight for the bathroom and slammed the door behind me. I leaned against the wall and slid to the floor and cried. For the animals. For the suffering in this world. For the fact that the smuggling will go on because I just screwed up. Dalton eased the door open and poked his head in.

"Go away," I said.

He sat down on the floor next to me and wrapped his arms around me. "It's all right," he whispered. "It'll be all right."

"I'm so sorry," I cried. "I screwed up big time. I blew

everything. I'm so sorry." My tears wet his shirt.

"Don't worry. I think they actually believed you. I think it'll be okay." He stroked my hair and I let loose and sobbed until I couldn't cry anymore.

"I just couldn't," I whimpered, my breath ragged as I tried to regain control. "I just couldn't—"

"I know," he soothed and rubbed my back. "I know."

"Oh my god, the horror. They were sitting in their own feces. The birds, their feathers ripped out."

"I know."

I sat back, rubbed my nose with the back of my hand, and faced him. "I was the top of my class. Hand to hand combat. I won the firearm medal. I aced the law exam, for chrissake. Why can't—" My eyes teared up again and the words caught in my throat. "Why can't I handle this?"

He didn't say anything. Not a dig, not an admonition, or even how to fix it. He just took me in his arms and held me some more.

"How do you do it?" I sniffled.

"You keep your mind focused on the big picture." His fingers twirled in my hair. "You play for the long game."

"But meanwhile, all those animals suffer."

He nodded. "We can't save them all."

"How can you stand it? We've gotta stop it. We've got to."

"We are." He patted my back. "Every moment we get closer."

"We've gotta go back." I jerked from his embrace. "We need to choose a monkey we can document, can identify, right? So when he smuggles it, we can bust him."

Dalton was shaking his head. "Listen to me. I told you before, we're not here to bust anyone. We're here to gather intel. Taking down someone so low on the totem pole will gain nothing."

"It'll gain something for those animals!" I huffed. "I memorized the route we took in the van. I can draw a map to that barn. We can stake it out."

"That's not our call to make. Do I need to remind you, we're not on U.S. soil? We're here under a special agreement. These are Costa Rican citizens. We have no authority for that."

"Then we call in the Fuerza Pública."

"It's not our mission."

"But we can't just ignore the, the horror of it."

"I know it's hard, but that's exactly what we do." He smiled at me, the smile of someone trying to make someone else's pain go away, then took me by the hand, pulling me to my feet, and led me out of the bathroom. We sat down on the edge of the bed. "We made a huge step forward tonight. This is the closest we've gotten." He rubbed a tear from my cheek with his thumb. "Smile. We did good."

"How can you say that?" I couldn't stand it. My teeth clenched involuntarily and I started to shake.

"Poppy, listen to me. If you want to work Special Ops, you have to accept the fact that this is what we do. It's not all about saving fuzzy bunnies. This is syndicated, organized crime. We slowly work our way in. We have to pass up the small players to go after the big fish. Sometimes it takes years."

I huffed. "Meanwhile, millions of animals suffer."

"Yes, millions of animals are suffering. But we can't save them overnight." He sighed. "You seem like a really passionate woman. With all respect, I'm not sure this kind of work is for you."

"Not for—" I held my breath. I wanted to scream, to gouge his eyes out, to set something on fire. "I've dedicated my life to this!"

Dalton held his hands up. "Whoa, hey."

"I could kick your ass."

He smirked. "No doubt."

"Now you're being an asshole!"

"I—" He threw up his hands. "I give up."

I crossed my arms and flopped back on the bed. The steam

fizzled from my head and I was spent. "All I've ever wanted to be, for as long as I can remember, is a wildlife cop."

He eased back onto the pillow beside me. Smiled. "Because you love animals so much."

I nodded. "My father—" I sniffled "—my father said I was born with a love for every creature on Earth." I closed my eyes. "He used to take me with him on photo shoots. He was a wildlife photographer."

"He sounds like a pretty cool dad."

I swallowed hard. I missed him so much. "He was."

Dalton said nothing.

"My mom was always gone, out to sea or somewhere. My dad homeschooled me. We lived wherever mom was stationed or in the forest near the animal he happened to be obsessed with."

"He did a fine job raising you."

In a faked stern voice I said, "Not a proper upbringing."

He grinned.

"I speak five languages. Learned them all from subtitles watching eighties reruns in whatever country we were in. My dad, he wanted me to be…" I held back the tears.

Dalton took my hand. "You're all that and more."

The damn tears started again. "People are so cruel."

"Listen, there's no shame in it." He cupped my face in his hands and made me look him in the eyes. "No shame in feeling what you're feeling." His eyes brightened and his lip turned up at the side. "It's beautiful, actually."

He pulled me toward him and I snuffled in his chest and cried some more.

I came awake slowly, with a warm, snuggly, safe feeling, like I was emerging from a cocoon. Too warm actually. I wasn't alone. I was cuddled against a man, my arm draped over his naked chest, my leg entwined with his leg. I sat up. *Crap!*

"Sorry, sorry," I babbled.

He smiled lazily and his eyes opened. "You're beautiful in the morning, you know that? With those rosy cheeks."

"Are you trying to make me feel better?"

His eyes turned lustful. "I'm trying to tell you that you're beautiful."

"Oh," I said. I didn't know what to do. "Thank you?"

He grinned. "You don't like compliments, do you?"

"I don't know. You could have mentioned my skill when I pinned you down with the thumb lock. Now that'd be a worthy compliment."

He shook his head. "You really are something." He rolled over and sat up on his side of the bed. He combed his fingers through his hair and rubbed his eyes. He was wearing boxers. I sneaked a look.

I went into the bathroom and stared at myself in the mirror. I was a mess. Dark circles under my eyes. My pupils ragged like a madman's. My red mop needed an overhaul with a professional pair of scissors. I grabbed handfuls of my hair. "Arrrgh! You need to get your head on straight," I said to my reflection.

I washed my face and ran a comb through my hair. Then I went back out and plopped on the bed next to Dalton. "I suppose you're going to send me home now."

"Actually, I was thinking, maybe this will be a good way for you to connect with Maria, you know, the lost baby thing."

"Now the wife?" I glared at him. "What is it with you?" *Damn, why am I being like this?*

He frowned. "Or yes, you can go home."

"I'm sorry," I said. "It's just that…well, just because I, last night I, you know, doesn't mean I'm not capable of helping with the real work here. I have skills. I'm as good as any man." I launched from the bed. "I bet you're one of those guys who thinks women shouldn't be in combat."

"Uh, yeah. Women shouldn't be in combat."

"I knew it. You think we aren't strong enough, aren't smart

enough. You think we can't handle it."

"I never said that."

"You got this macho frogman ego. Elitist military crap. You know what I've got? The element of surprise. No one suspects little 'ol me. I can sashay right in and bam, knock you on your ass. I can outshoot you any day. Line up some cans, buddy."

"You know what I'm picturing right now," he said. "Me with my hand on your head and you swinging in the air."

"You are such an asshole!"

"You're so cute when you get all riled up."

"Cute? I'm cute!"

"Yes, my lovely, beautiful, cute little bride." He smirked. "Get it? I know you don't like it, but you're the wife. That's your role here. Take it or leave it."

I clenched down on my teeth so hard I thought my molars might shatter. "Yes. Thank you," I said. I'd rather stick an icepick in my eye, but there it was. My directive—be a good wife. *Shoot me now!* "Maybe I can learn to play bridge and make a positively delicious soufflé."

"Now you're talking," he said. He shuffled around the room, looking for his phone. He called George and all I heard on this end was an occasional yeah or uh-huh. He hung up. "He wants me to play cards tonight. I'll be late. Take the time to get your head together. Go to the beach, go to a spa. Whatever."

Like hell. I had something else in mind.

CHAPTER 9

I stopped by the butterfly gardens. He wasn't there. I went straight to the tree house. Noah was stretched out in the hammock, playing his guitar, an old Johnny Cash tune. I called up. "May I come in?"

He glanced down at me and my insides went squishy. God, he was yummy. He flashed a grin and I steeled myself. No kissing this time. I took the stairs two at a time. He eyed me from the hammock, but didn't get up. "Wasn't sure if I'd see you again," he said, matter-of-fact.

"Yeah, about that. Sorry?"

"I'm glad you're here now," he said and leaned forward and set down his guitar. "You look like you've got something on your mind."

"Haven't been able to get it off my mind actually. What you were saying, about the wildlife poachers."

"Oh, you were listening. Your first mistake," he said with a grin. He wiggled his empty beer bottle at me. "What can I get you?"

"Um, I'm not really a beer for breakfast kinda gal."

"Wine then?"

"Ah, sure." One glass wouldn't hurt.

Noah slipped across the hanging bridge, which I now saw led to a kitchen. He came back with two stemmed glasses in one hand and a corkscrew and a bottle of red in the other. "I figure you for a red kinda gal. Am I right?"

I smiled. He was right. I did a quick double take. The bottle in his hand was a $150 vintage. "So what's your story?" I asked. "All I know about you is that you volunteer at the butterfly gardens and in your spare time you like to dodge bullets."

"Yeah, well, don't let the Superman costume fool you. That was a pretty foolish thing to do." He handed me a glass (poured one-third full, the way it should be done) and held his up to mine. By the stem. "Here's to a little foolishness," he said.

"Indeed," I said, my eyes meeting his as we clinked our glasses together. Oh, what the hell. I leaned into him for a kiss.

"Mmmm," he said. "I like this vintage." He kissed me again until I was breathless, then pulled away. "You know what I think?" he said.

I held my breath.

"You're trying to woo me with your sexy wiles."

I grinned. "Woo you? Seriously? Who says that?"

"My grandma." He shrugged. "Of course, she was bat shit crazy."

"So you got it from her?"

He raised his glass as if to salute her in thanks. "You got it, babe," he said and took a sip. "Every bat shit crazy chromosome."

"How crazy are you?" I asked.

His gaze turned heavy. "What'd you have in mind?"

"I want to set those animals free. Every one of them. I don't care about video tapes and ticking off the guards. Supply and demand be damned. I don't care about the law either. It's all bullshit anyway. I want those animals out of that barn and back in the wild where they belong."

"Okay," he said. "I like a woman who knows what she wants."

"I'm serious."

"I am, too." He poured more wine. "So what did you have in

mind? I can call the gang, get them over here."

"No," I said. The more people involved, the more risky it would be. "Just me and you. Tonight."

He raised his eyebrows. "I like the sound of that."

"So no more wine." I set my glass down.

His lips turned up into an exaggerated pout. "What about one more kiss?"

I drew in a breath. He had my kryptonite. He set down his glass and moved toward me, his eyes on my lips. My pulse leaped into overdrive. Why'd he have to be so hot? His kisses so, damn, wow—I tilted my head back and he nuzzled my neck. He looked up at me and my eyes flitted toward the bed. "We could always storm the shed tomorrow night," he whispered, his hand moving from my waist to my backside and down.

"No," I said, pulling away. "Tonight. They can't be in those cages one more night."

"All right, all right," he said. He took a step back and held up his hands in surrender. "Tonight it is."

Our plan was simple. Sneak in under the cover of darkness, deal with the guards, release the animals. We agreed—violence wasn't acceptable. Taking out the guards needed some finesse. Distraction? Perhaps. Deal with them one at a time, tying them up? Could get dicey.

"I have an idea," Noah said. He picked up his phone. "I need a favor," he said when his call was answered. "Where are you?" A moment later he disconnected and said to me, "I'll be back." And he was gone.

I reclined in the rattan chair with my glass of wine. Why let it go to waste, right? Especially a Chateau Montelena. I stared at the label. What twenty-something year old guy, who lives in a tree house in Costa Rica and volunteers at the butterfly garden, can casually serve a $150 bottle of wine? He hadn't given any other indication of trying to impress me with money.

If anything, he'd been doing the opposite. His friends were all down to Earth, good-hearted folks. No one was knocking down six figures back in the States. They'd all freely talked about their jobs. Except Noah.

My heart was all in, but my head, or more specifically my training, urged me to find out more.

I wandered down the rope bridge to the kitchen. It was a wooden platform surrounded by a half wall about eight feet above the ground. A propane cooktop, oven, and chopping block lined one side, a sink built into the home-made counter top on the other. Nothing unique or extraordinary. I continued down the stairs to the shed below. An open padlock hung from the door latch. I eased the door open and stepped inside to find a state-of-the-art refrigerator, the kind that's highly energy efficient, a critter-proof cabinet stocked with gourmet foods, and, built into the sandy ground like a bunker, a wine cellar that could grace the pages of *Wine Aficionado*. At least two-hundred bottles lined the walls.

I backed out of the shed and pushed the door back to the position in which I had found it. Back up the stairs, I poked around some more. Clothes, shoes, underwear. Boxer-briefs. I paused, imagining him in them. I shoved the drawer shut. Beside the bed, a tiny built-in door hung askew. It seemed out of place. I eased it open to find a solid door to a safe behind. I snapped the door back shut, making sure it hung in the same crooked angle and went back to my glass of wine.

He could be a trust-funder like Claudia had suggested. That would explain the modesty. But generally, in my experience, someone who spends that much on a bottle of wine does so because he feels he's earned it. It didn't fit.

Noah came bounding up the stairs with a tiny travel case in his hands. He popped it open to display the contents, a sneaky grin on his face. "What do you think?" Eight sedative injection darts were clipped into the case, each large enough for a big predator. "The dart gun's in the van."

"My god, that dose looks like enough to take down an elephant. That's crazy."

"Jaguars, actually. I like to think of it as poetic justice." He flashed that grin again and my heart skipped a beat.

It wasn't ideal, but it was a non-violent approach. "I guess we're all set then," I said. "Now we just have to wait for dark."

He reached for his guitar. "I take requests." A monkey zipped up the railing and into the hammock. "Hey Clyde," said Noah. He turned to me. "Watch out. He likes the vino."

I tipped my glass and downed the last sip. Clyde leaped to the railing, wrapped his tail around it, pulled the hammock up to him, then leaped on. As it swung back and forth, he chittered and peeped with glee. When the hammock slowed, he jumped up and got it swinging again.

"His favorite toy," said Noah.

I looked down the stairs. "Where's Isabella?"

"She lives in one of the houses here on the property. Clyde comes and goes." He went to the bathroom and came back with something in his hand. He tossed it into the air and Clyde caught it with the skill of a miniature wide receiver. "It's a monkey biscuit. They're like Flintstones for monkeys. He loves 'em. I have to keep them in there, though, because it's the only place he can't get. He can't work the round door handle with only one good hand."

"Sounds like he can be a little stinker."

"That's putting it mildly."

Clyde held the biscuit in a tight grip, his one nimble little hand against the tiny stump of his right, as he gnawed away, crumbs cascading to the floor. His eyes flitted about, looking for other monkeys I assumed. Crunch, crunch, crunch and it was gone. He bounced up and down, flailing his little arms and chittering.

"Clean up your crumbs," Noah told him. "He wants another one." He pointed at the pile of crumbs on the floor. "Clean 'em up."

Clyde chittered away, whining like a toddler.

"Not until you clean up that mess," Noah said, shaking his head.

Clyde slunk to the floor, swept up the crumbs with his hand, licked them off his fingers, then sprang back up to the edge of the hammock and squealed for another biscuit.

"All right, one more," Noah said and went to the bathroom. Clyde spun around, jumping up and down with excitement. Noah lobbed the biscuit into the air and Clyde scrambled up the hammock line, up the support post, grabbed a ceiling truss, and flung himself into the air, catching the biscuit in mid air before he landed on the coffee table.

"He's too cute," I said. After he finished his second biscuit, he crawled onto my lap and curled up into a ball. "Wow, I can't get over how he's a completely different monkey than the one I met at the bar."

"Yeah, drunk people can be unpredictable and cruel. He knows he's safe here."

I gently petted him and he cooed.

"He's been a good bar monkey, though. He's never bit anyone."

I held him in my arms, enjoying him cuddling with me, and thought of the newlyweds at the bar. How was I any different? It was a cruel catch twenty-two. People who love animals are the ones who drive the industry. They simply don't understand that for their two minutes of enjoyment with the animal, that animal endures a lifetime of subjugation and, often, cruelty. The brutal truth is that breaking a wild animal's spirit to a point that it will accept interaction with people usually means beating them, or worse. It's not the natural way of things.

I rubbed Clyde under his muzzle. "I'm so sorry, little buddy," I whispered. I thought of the monkeys I'd met last night and my pulse quickened. I shook my head. "I won't let it happen to them," I said to Clyde. "Your cousins are going to be free."

I turned to Noah, my mind back on the plan and getting

prepared. Yesterday, when I was at the shed, I'd been too focused on my purpose—to choose the monkey. But now, as I recalled the scene and the layout of the shed, I remembered that besides the stacks of cages, there were two large iron contraptions in the shed. They looked like rusty old exploding mines from World War One. "What can you tell me about the layout of the shed? Have you ever been inside?" I asked. "I'd like to know what's there."

"We've only made the attempt a few times. We have Claudia's video. And Clyde's. Both are not very good footage."

"Can I see them anyway?"

"Sure," he said. He opened the safe in the wall and pulled out a laptop. (So that's what was in there.) He fired it up and found the videos right away. They were too dark, difficult to see the animals at all, but the contraptions were visible. "Pause right there," I said. "What are those?"

"Old ball coffee roasters. The huge iron ball is filled with coffee beans and slowly turned over a hot fire, to roast them evenly, kinda like a rotisserie popcorn popper. See the crank and the turning wheel? Underneath here"—he pointed—"is where they'd build the fire."

"Looks like a giant version of the little buddy burner I made with my dad when I was a girl."

Noah got a silly grin on his face. "You were a Girl Scout?"

I ignored him. "Is this some kind of heat shield then?" The second one must have been the same roaster with the shield closed. It looked like a giant oil drum with the turning wheel sticking out the side.

"Yeah. The heat shield surrounds the whole thing like an exoskeleton."

My turn to grin. "You're really a bug guy at heart, aren't you?"

He raised his hands in mock surrender. "Guilty."

We left the van in the same pull off, which meant we had a two-hour hike up the side of the mountain. Noah carried a GPS unit but seemed to know exactly where he was going. I followed, carrying the dart gun. I wasn't sure if he'd ever shot anything before, so I convinced him to let me do the shooting.

The jungle was alive with the incessant chitter of countless insects mixed with the occasional low-pitched thrum of nocturnal creatures bounding through the canopy. "Costa Rica is home to more than 500,000 species of critters, about 300,000 of which are insects," said Noah. "894 birds, around 175 amphibians, approximately 225 reptiles, and nearly 250 mammals, including the elusive jaguar—a nocturnal hunter."

"Yeah, I'd like to avoid each and every one of them," I said. "Especially the snakes." The key was watching our step and making our presence known. Unfortunately, this conflicted with our goal of a surprise attack.

As we approached the compound, we moved silently and cautiously. Then Noah motioned for me to halt. "There's usually a guard at that corner," he said. "Something's up."

An important rule of the tactical ambush is to know your enemy's movement and positions. An unaccounted-for guard is a serious problem. He could be in the latrine, changing shifts, or standing behind you with a gun aimed at your head. "Let's check the other positions, then circle back," I said.

We moved single file through the jungle, avoiding the bell alarms. Of the usual five guards, we could see only two who paced at the entrance looking bored. "Maybe they're taking the night off," Noah said.

I shook my head. "I don't like it."

"What do you want to do?"

Maybe they only kept two guards at night. That didn't seem out of the realm of possibility.

"I say we go for it," he said. "We're here now. And all those animals are in there."

I moved to get a better look. One guard was tipping a bottle to his mouth, then handed it to the other. Perfect. You don't share your Coca-Cola. Moonshine plus a jaguar-size dose of sedative ought to do the trick for sure.

"At least they're standing near each other," Noah said. "You can hit them one right after the other."

I waited until both were turned and facing the other way, then raised the dart gun, aimed and fired. The first guard reached for his butt cheek and started to crumple. I reloaded and fired again. The second guard slowly slumped forward.

We waited in the shadows for a full five minutes, watching for another guard to come along. I told Noah to wait where he was and circled the entire shed one more time to be sure no one else lurked about, then we crept out into the open, toward the men.

While Noah plucked the darts from their butts, I checked their pulses. Snoozing like babies. We propped them up beside each other with the bottle in the one man's hand. Not the first time a bad jag on moonshine made for a foggy memory.

The shed was dark, normally a sign that no one was inside, but we needed to be extra cautious. With the dart gun reloaded and at the ready (the only weapon we had), we slipped inside the door. Noah reached for the switch, gave it a flip, and the tubes flickered to life.

I stared in disbelief. The shed was empty. Every animal. Every cage. Gone.

I spun around and shined my flashlight on the ground outside the door. Fresh tire tracks in the dirt. "Dammit! A shipment must have gone out today."

"No wonder there were only two guards."

I turned back around and more slowly scanned the shed, my brain not fully accepting the situation. It was empty save for two folding chairs, a large workbench along the wall, and in the back corner, the two large coffee roasters.

"We need to get out of here. Now," I said.

"Wait," Noah said. "Check this out."

Strewn across the top of the counter where he stood were

tiny pieces of rubber or plastic. I picked one up and twirled it between my fingers. A burst balloon maybe or a condom. One side was coated in a white powder.

Crap. This complicates everything.

Then we heard a sound outside. Noah and I looked at each other. It was the sound of hoofbeats.

We were standing in the center of an empty shed, with the lights on. Sitting ducks. I glanced at the coffee roasters. It was our only option. I gestured for Noah to follow.

"¿Qué es esto?" *What is this?* A woman's voice outside. "Levántense, hombres perezosos." *Get up you lazy men.*

Hiding behind the roaster wouldn't provide enough cover; a simple walk around and we'd be caught. We gently opened the heat shield on the roaster furthest from the door, squeezed inside, and as we pulled the shield shut the hinge creaked, the rubbing of rusty iron on iron. My heart pounded in my chest.

Footsteps crossed the concrete floor. Then the clickety, clickety, click of tiny dog feet. "¿Qué puñetas está pasando?" *What the hell is going on?*

Maria? What was she doing up here?

The dogs came straight to the roaster and yipped. I looked at Noah. *We're screwed.*

"Ya basta!" she hollered. *Knock it off!* The dogs retreated. The footsteps circled, then paced back. "Dammit!" Then the beeps of a cell phone being dialed. "¿Qué te he dicho sobre el tráfico de drogas?" *What have I told you about running drugs?* A pause. "Dammit!" The beeps of her dialing again. "Es un pecado, Carlos. Un pecado contra Dios!" *It's a sin, Carlos. A sin against God!* There was a long pause. "Tú no vas a poner en peligro mi operación de nuevo." *You will not jeopardize my operation again.* "¿Me entiendes, hermano?"

Hermano. Brother. Carlos was Maria's brother. But she said *my* operation. *Holy crap! Maria is the kingpin.*

The lights switched off and Noah and I were trapped in the roaster in the pitch dark.

CHAPTER 10

I waited a full two minutes before I whispered in his ear, "We have to get out of here before the guards wake up."

At least Maria had switched off the lights and we had the cover of darkness. We eased the heat shield back, slipped from the roaster, and tiptoed to the door. The guards were still out cold. I took one step and saw the horse, tied to a post. She was still here. But where? I backed up and stepped on Noah's foot. He stumbled backward but caught me and we regained our balance. I sidestepped away from the door, dragging him with me. "The horse," I whispered.

"Where could she be?"

I shook my head. There wasn't much here save for the shed. Then I remembered. The basket on the cable. I leaned out and peered into the darkness. I caught sight of a light beam among the foliage. "She's gone up the path," I whispered. "There's an old cable car up there."

"Yeah," Noah said. "To the outhouse. Could we be so lucky?"

"Let's get the hell out of here while we can."

"I agree," he said and darted across the yard into the jungle. I was right on his heels.

I needed to think, to regroup. I made excuses and left Noah as quickly as I could.

When I got to the bungalow, Dalton wasn't back from the card game yet.

I sat down in the chair and tried to settle my mind. Deep breaths. Ommmmmm.

I jumped up from the chair. That wasn't going to work. Okay. I paced.

All right. Maria's the kingpin. She's running the show. Not George. Why would she ride her horse all the way up to the shed at 11:30 at night? In the pitch dark? She would have known the shed was empty. Wouldn't she? Was she checking on Carlos? Maybe she had suspected the drugs and wanted to catch him?

That explains why George had all the buyers to dinner at the house. *So she could approve us without anyone realizing.* It made perfect sense.

How was I going to prove it? I needed to catch her red-handed. But doing what exactly? Dalton had made it very clear he wasn't interested in catching her offering a sale. He wanted confirmation she was the kingpin. That was it. How would I get that? She'd kept her identity hidden well.

The only thing I knew for sure: I couldn't tell Dalton any of this. He couldn't know I'd sneaked up there to that shed. He'd kill me. That also meant I couldn't get his help. I was going to have to figure it out on my own.

I'd play the wife. Make Dalton happy. See what I could find out. Maybe I could press for the horseback riding, or stop by to visit with no excuse. Women do that all the time, don't they? But Maria wasn't the type to tolerate a mousy wife coming around wanting to chitchat. I wouldn't get many chances.

And I didn't have much time. I would have to force her to come to me, to show her hand somehow. But how?

She certainly was arrogant, sure of herself. Maybe I could use that to my advantage. She was smart, that was sure. She'd come up with a pretty good arrangement to keep herself hidden. She'd been right under Nash and Dalton's noses. I needed some way to lure her out, to force her to expose herself. But what? How?

I went into the bathroom and looked in the mirror. "You can do this. You can do anything you set your mind to."

Then it wasn't my voice I was hearing, but my dad's. I was holding a salamander in my five-year-old hands, a smile spread across my face. I raised it proudly, showing off my new pet. *Oh Poppy,* he said. *Sweetheart, you can't keep him. He needs to stay in the wild.* But Daddy, I pleaded, already knowing he wouldn't be swayed. I've made a home for him. Look. I pointed to the shoebox with the mound of sand, the pile of leaves, the butter dish of water. He'll be happy with me. *C'mere,* he said and patted the top of his thighs. I sat down on his lap. He poked at my chest. *You've got a big, beautiful, loving heart. Right now, that's what you're thinking with. And that's okay. That's how we love. But taking care of Mr. Salamander here takes a lot more than love. You need to use your head, too. You see, he's not meant to live in a box. He needs the entire eco-system to survive. He can't survive without it, and it can't live without him. Do you understand?* My dad took me by the hand and we walked together, back to the muddy bank where I'd found the salamander and I set it down and watched it slink behind a moss-covered log, tears spilling down my cheeks. *Oh, don't be sad, Sweetheart,* my daddy said. *You just made him the happiest salamander alive. He's safe now, at home, with his family.* But I can't live without him, Daddy. *You can,* he said. *You can do anything you set your mind to.*

"You can do this," I said again to the face in the mirror. This was my way into Special Ops. I had to make it happen. "Find a way."

But no matter how I did it, Dalton wasn't going to like it. I crossed my arms. So be it. Sometimes it's easier to beg forgiveness than to ask permission.

"Tomorrow, Maria, I'm going to take you down."

"I'm taking the day off to spend with my visiting wife," Dalton said before taking a gulp of his orange juice.

"What? No. You were right." *Why is this happening now?* "I need to get over there and make friends with Maria. I shouldn't waste any time."

"Tomorrow," he said. "My wife came all the way down here from Texas. I need to spend time with her."

"Seems like a waste of precious time you could be spending with George. What if you miss something important?"

"It's more important to be true to our cover. We are going to the beach together, snorkeling, surfing, whatever you want to do." He picked up his fork. "And the best part—" he raised his eyebrows "—is I get to see you in a bikini."

I frowned. Men. *Dammit!* I had plans to make, things to do. I had to figure this out. And I was stuck with Dalton, sitting by the pool like a couple of tourists.

I watched the colorful finches and tanagers flit to and fro, devouring the fruit that had been set out on a platform feeder as I finished my yogurt trying to figure out how to thwart his plan.

"Relax," said Dalton, a greasy chicken thigh in his fingers. "Most of the time this job demands our all. We don't get to choose. Every minute of our day we're on, you know what I mean. Let's go have some fun. It's what John and Brittany are supposed to be doing today. Might as well enjoy it."

I nodded, trying to appear agreeable.

I got up to refill my coffee and stopped dead.

"There you are!" My friend Chris was coming across the patio, his arms wide. *Oh crap!* "Girl, you are hard to track down." He wrapped his arms around me.

I hugged him back and put my lips to his ear. "Call me Brittany," was all I could get out before I had to break from the embrace without causing attention. I wasn't sure if he heard me. I smiled. "What a surprise." I gestured toward Dalton. "Chris, this is my husband, John." Chris's eyes grew large. He looked at Dalton, up and down, then back to me, his mouth hanging open.

"So you ran off and got hitched, huh? Lordy, girl, I never would've thunk it. Well, that explains you being my bestie *in absentia*."

I glanced at Dalton. He looked so mad I thought his hair might catch on fire. He smiled through clenched teeth as he rose and reached out to shake Chris's hand. I glanced around the patio and saw Yipes. He seemed to just notice us. "Listen," I said to Chris. "This isn't a good time."

"What? I just got here." He grabbed the back of a chair and pulled it out to sit down.

Dalton growled, "I'll be in the bungalow. You've got two minutes," then lumbered away.

"What a grumpy, grump," Chris said. "I mean, I know I surprised you but—"

"Chris, listen to me—"

"Married? How could you not tell me?" He turned to me and I thought I had his attention, but he kept on. "No wonder you were in a tizzy." He held up his hands. "I get it. You wanted to tell me in person. Geez, and I thought my news was spectacular." He ran his hand down his silk shirt. "I got a raise. Check out my new duds. Genuine—"

"Chris, shut the hell up and listen to me."

He jerked back like he'd been slapped. "All right, already."

I leaned in close. "I'm undercover and you're going to screw it up. Do you understand?"

"No kidding?" He glanced around. "Are we being watched right now?"

"I need you to go. Now."

"Okay, okay," he said, smiling a fake smile and nervously brushing imaginary lint from his silk shirt.

"Are you staying at that place you mentioned, the one with the swim up bar?"

"Yeah, Coco-Cabana." He pursed his lips. "So you aren't married?"

"I'll call you there when I can, okay?"

"Yeah, sure. Of course you're not. Sorry, man. I didn't know." He shrugged. "I was worried about you."

"I'm sorry. This was my fault." I gave him a reassuring smile. "I like the shirt. But the chain and the white fedora," I cringed. "Too much. You look like a drug dealer."

He tugged at his collar, making sure it laid the way he wanted. "Yeah, well, that's the look I was going for." He turned on his heel and shuffled off.

As I stepped into the room, Dalton was hanging up the phone. "Pack your bag," he said with an unsettling calm.

"Dalton, I didn't—"

"Doesn't matter."

"But I—"

"It doesn't matter."

I stared at him. He wasn't going to budge. "How are you—"

"Your mother's sick. Needs you right away. I got you a seat on a plane this afternoon." He crossed his arms. "You'd better hurry to the airport."

I nodded. "Yes, sir." *Argh!*

I picked up the phone and dialed the cab company. "They'll be here in fifteen minutes," I said. "Will you please return the moped then?" I went to the bathroom and got my toiletries bag. Everything else was already in my suitcase. I sat down on the edge of the bed and sighed. All my dreams, devastated by one weak moment, one phone call to a friend. *Dammit!* At least I figured out who the kingpin was. At least I'd done that much. I glowered at Dalton. "It's Maria."

"What are you talking about?" he said.

"Maria. She's the kingpin."

He looked at me with skeptical eyes. "How do you know this?"

"The palapa bar, The Toucan. The one in the postcard. I found out Carlos Mendoza is the owner, he—"

"You went to the bar?" He threw up his hands. "Dammit, Poppy."

"His family owns the land that abuts George's property. It was him at the shed. "

"Yeah, so?"

"Maria and Carlos are brother and sister."

He stared at me. I could tell he was turning it over in his mind. "It's a connection to George. Doesn't mean she's involved."

How could I make him believe me? "But it all makes sense. You know George isn't—"

"Okay, enough. I've heard enough."

"It's her, Dalton. We gotta stop her."

"We aren't doing anything." He got up and grabbed my suitcase. "You're getting on a plane."

"But I—"

He flung open the door and shoved the suitcase at me. "Just go." He hustled me out and slammed the door behind me. The air left my body. So that was it. It was over. I slinked to a nearby bench and sat down to wait for the taxi. I wanted to storm back inside, tell him everything, tell him how I knew, but he probably wouldn't believe me anyway. I had no proof.

When the taxi pulled into the drive, I slid into the back seat, hugging my damn over-sized purse against me. "Aeropuerto, por favor," I said and slammed my head back.

The driver put the cab in gear, drove out of the drive and on to the main road and I felt everything slip away. All because, in a moment of frustration, I had needed a friend. *Dammit!*

The taxi moved along in traffic, then suddenly the driver jerked the vehicle to the side of the road.

I sat upright. "¿Qué pasa?" I asked.

"Meep, meep, meep!" Came the silly horn of a moped behind us. Why on earth would he pull over for a moped? I spun around in my seat.

Dalton was knocking on the side window. He opened the cab door, grabbed my hand, and pulled me from the back seat.

"I'm sorry, darling. I love you. Say you'll stay." He wrapped his arms around me and plastered me with kisses. "Let's not ever fight again."

"I'm sorry, too," I said and kissed him on the mouth. "Take me to bed or lose me forever." He dug in his pocket and tossed a few dollars at the grinning cabbie, grabbed my suitcase, and slammed the door shut.

"Pura vida, mis amigos," said the cab driver as he pulled away.

Dalton swung a leg over the moped and I tried to fit onto the seat behind him, my obnoxious white leather suitcase balanced on my knee. Dalton made a U-turn and we puttered back to the bungalow.

Once inside the room, I asked, "What's going on?"

He stared at me, paced, then stared at me again as though he was still trying to decide whether he should have left me in the cab. He thrust his hands on his hips and said, "I think you, well, my gut tells me...what I mean to say is, I think you might be right. I've had the same suspicions."

I assessed him for a moment. "Why? What have you seen?"

"It doesn't matter. What you say makes sense. And since—" He gritted his teeth. "Dammit!"

"Dammit what?" *He's not telling me everything. He's holding something back.*

"Brittany would want to connect with the wife, right? That'd be natural." He paused, then through clenched teeth, said, "We have to see it through."

I tried to hide my excitement. "I'm telling you, Dalton. It's her. I know it's—"

"Yeah." He had his hand up to shush me as he shuffled across the room, picked up his phone, and dialed George. After their hellos, he chuckled and said, "You know how women are. She's been on my back about horseback riding with Maria." I felt like we were kids and he was scheduling a playdate. "Yeah, uh-huh." There was a long pause. "All right. Thanks." And he disconnected.

"He said to come on over."

I grinned. "Dalton, I swear—"

"You've got three days to see what you can find out. Then we both get on a plane and go home. I'll be making the next run alone. Do you understand me? Three days." He made sure he had my attention. "But you listen to me, you better watch your step. This reckless behavior of yours has got to stop. From now on, you do as I say, do you understand?"

I nodded.

"You don't go anywhere, you don't do anything, you don't talk to anybody without my approval. You got it?"

"Yes," I said, my expression solemn. "I got it."

He eyed me for a long moment. He didn't believe me. It was all right. Neither did I.

"Sit down. We've got a half an hour to get you prepped."

I did as he commanded.

"Your first priority is to gain her trust. Don't ask her a lot of questions. You are the clueless, sweet, loving wife. You wanted a pet monkey is all. You have no idea it's illegal." He rubbed his chin. "But don't talk about that unless she brings it up. Understand?"

I shook my head. "No illegal monkey talk."

"Make it seem like we've got a lot of rich friends. Don't be blatant about it, but make it part of who you are, a wealthy socialite with filthy rich friends."

"Rich friends. Okay."

"It's all right to have different opinions, disagree with her, whatever. Don't ingratiate yourself. It could cause suspicion."

I nodded.

"Are you listening to me?"

"Every word."

He sighed and combed his fingers through his hair. "This op is turning to shit." He looked me in the eye. "Are you sure you can handle this?"

"I know I screwed up before. And I never should have called Chris. I just—I can do this. You can trust me."

"I hope so," he said. "Now, you're going horseback riding, so—"

I opened my eyes wide and let my mouth drop open. "Oh my god, I have to get on a horse?"

He closed his eyes. "Oh, we're screwed."

"Dalton, I'm kidding."

He glared at me. "If they don't kill you, I might."

CHAPTER 11

I left on the moped, Dalton in the car. He was going to golf with George.

I figured I could get away with a few extra minutes so I parked near the beach, two hotels down from the Coco-Cabana. I found Chris lounging by the pool with a piña colada in his hand, his eyeballs glued to a team of college boys in the pool playing volleyball over a tiny net.

When he saw me, he sprang to his feet. "Oh my god, girl. Did I get you fired? I am so sorry."

"Don't worry about it. I told you, it was my fault."

"Man. If I'd a known."

"I smoothed it over." I scanned the pool crowd. I didn't want to run into anyone else I might know. "How long are you planning to stay?"

His eyes traveled back to the bare chested guys in the pool. "Honey, I might never leave." A blond spiked the ball and it hit the side of the pool and bounced across the patio. "I've got it," Chris yelled and scurried to pick it up.

"You're incorrigible, you know that?" I said when he returned.

"Yes, but I get laid a lot more than you do, my dear." He smacked me with a kiss on the lips. "You look exhausted." He sat down in his lounge chair and patted the one next to it. "Take a load off." He hailed the waiter walking by with a tray full of tropical libations. "I'll order one with an umbrella. That way, as you sip it, you won't have to worry about burning that little pink nose."

Chris had that creamy olive skin of the perfect mix of genes. His mother was Egyptian, his father of Scandinavian descent. No one could guess where he was from. He fit in anywhere on the globe, sunny or otherwise.

I shook my head. "I can't. I've gotta go."

"At least tell me about that hunk of meat you are shacking up with. This fake husband. Is there any fake sex going on? Give me the juice." His eyes went back to the blond in the pool. "I mean, he's not really my type, but I can see why you got all flustered and had to call."

"He's my partner. And this job…" I slumped into the chair. "I've got a lot on my mind."

"Poppy-girl, you know how you are. You take on too much."

I looked at Chris, my best friend for as long as I can remember. His eyes were creased with worry. "I'm just frustrated really. This case." I took a deep breath. "At home, poaching, it's black and white. I catch you, you go to jail. But this." I shook my head. "It's complicated, organized crime. Even if I could catch someone red-handed, they'd get a slap on the wrist. That's why criminals choose it over running drugs. The risk is low, and for the big boys, the payoff high."

"Then the laws need to be changed." He held up his drink. "Maybe you should run for congress."

"Yeah, right. You've seen me in a suit."

"You'll find a way." Chris gave me a sympathetic frown. "Hey, they got Al Capone on tax evasion."

I stared at him, my mouth hanging open, recoiling from the jolt of an idea snapping into shape in my head. "You're a genius." *Yes, this could work.* Maria was one arrogant bitch who was used to being in control. But to do that, she required a lot of information. She had people watching our every move, had all the information about us at her fingertips. Or at least she thought she did.

I'd been so worried about Chris appearing, how it had looked to Yipes, I hadn't considered it might be useful in my favor. I ran over the scene in my mind, Dalton storming out, what Yipes thought he saw, different ways it could be interpreted. It was perfect.

"Hey, Earth to Poppy," Chris said, snapping me back to the now.

"I'm going to need a favor while you're here." Chris could do his part, then hop a plane out of here.

"So lay it on me."

"I need to get some information first, see if I can pull it together." I got up from the chair, my brain on fire, ideas spilling out. "But don't, whatever you do, come back by the bungalow, okay? I'll come here as soon as I can and fill you in." I took a step, then turned back. "And make sure you call me Brittany."

"Are you sure you're okay?"

"I'll be fine," I said and bent down and kissed him on the cheek. "Trust me."

"Yeah, right. The last time you said that I ended up with a shaved head and a case of the crabs."

The relative humidity had dropped. A cool breeze blew down from the mountain. The sky was dappled with big, white, puffy clouds. A beautiful day for a horseback ride.

Maria was filling a water bottle in the kitchen when I arrived. "Thank you so much for the invitation," I said. "I'm looking forward to a ride. It's been awhile since I've been out."

She forced a smile.

I shifted my weight to my other foot. "Have you been riding long?" I asked.

"Since I was a child," she said, in perfect Midwestern

English, no detectable Costa Rican accent.

"What a relief," I said, letting out my breath.

She looked at me quizzically.

"I thought maybe you didn't speak English."

She nodded as though that made sense. She handed me a water bottle. "The horses are being saddled."

I followed her and her little dogs to the barn. Once inside, I had to hide my surprise. The barn was immaculate. The floors swept clean, not one piece of straw out of place. Tack hung on hooks in front of each of eight sturdily built stalls. The horses looked clean and healthy. A hint of straw was the only odor I could detect. This was the barn of a wealthy equestrian who cared about her horses. It didn't fit the image I held of an evil wildlife smuggler—filthy cages, worm-ridden food. Interesting. As Noah had said: *Know thy enemy.*

A man I didn't recognize stood at the far door, arms crossed. The way his belt pulled tight at his waist, I was sure he had a firearm tucked at the small of his back.

Two horses were saddled, one with little saddle bags for Maria's dogs. Strange. Not an iota of guilt over the animals she tortures and sells, but she treats those little dogs like they're her children.

The horses were ready, but I had the sense we weren't going anywhere right away.

"I'm glad we are alone," Maria said. "I've been wanting to ask you something."

I shrugged. "Sure, shoot." *What is she up to?*

"Tell me, how do you say butterfly in Spanish?"

"Butterfly?" I asked. *Where is she going with this?*

"Yes, the beautiful insect with colorful wings."

"Um, mariposa?"

"Ah, yes, mariposa." The corners of her mouth curled into a devious smile. "It's funny. When my American friends try to learn Spanish, they always stumble on certain pronunciations."

Crap. Mari, rhymes with sorry. A newbie would pronounce it like Mary.

"You know what I think?" she said. She picked up a riding crop. "I think you are much smarter than you let on." Her intense gaze was intended to make me feel like a butterfly pinned to the wall.

I grinned wide and let out a sigh. "Oh thank god, you are a breath of fresh air," I said. Her eyes narrowed. She wasn't expecting this response. *Good.* "I thought I was going to be stuck with some woman who wanted to swap cookie recipes." I waved my hand in the air as if to dismiss her concern. "You know how men are—delicate egos." I leaned toward her as if to emphasize a secret. "Please don't tell John that I speak Spanish. He already feels like an idiot because he was an absolute dolt the other night when we got to talking about the wine." I rolled my eyes. "It's like he has to be good at everything or he doesn't feel like a man."

"Yes, well—" she smiled wide, a fake smile, and nodded to the man at the door "—your secret is safe with me. Shall we?" She moved toward her horse.

She was already dismissing me. This might be my only chance. *It's all or nothing.* "My husband, well, he doesn't exactly have a mind for business either. Oh, he's fine to look at, and oh my, in the sack—" I paused as if to savor a memory of our passionate lovemaking. "After awhile, a girl gets bored when there's not much upstairs, if you know what I mean. But in this misogynistic world, to do business, we women still need our men out front, even though we're the ones doing all the work. The brains behind the brawn, so to speak. If you know what I mean." I paused for effect, looked her straight in the eye. "But, of course, you know exactly what I mean."

She shifted her stance, ever so slightly. "Excuse me?"

I took a step closer to her. A subconscious sign of taking control. I lowered my voice. "I have no interest in one damn monkey. And I'm not looking for some amateur strap-a-bird-under-your-pants smuggler crap. I've got buyers, buyers with very big wallets. I want a source. A direct, reliable source."

Her eyes narrowed the slightest bit. Barely perceptible. She was good. "What you are describing sounds illegal. I think you have misunderstood. My husband's—"

"It's all right." I shrugged. "I'm sure I'll find what I'm looking for while I'm here in beautiful Costa Rica, nature's paradise." I winked. "Speaking of that. I must decline the ride. Enjoy yourself though. I've got business to attend to."

I turned my back on her and walked out the door.

I got back to the bungalow a couple hours before Dalton. Time to squeeze in some needed yoga.

"How'd it go?" he asked before the door was shut.

"Fine," I said.

"Fine? What does fine mean?"

I shrugged. "Fine. Nothing much to tell. She's cold. She didn't really want to take me. I think maybe George pressured her to, or she is covering her bases, keeping an eye on me. I don't know."

"Well, what'd you talk about?"

"Not much. We rode. Not a great situation for long conversations."

He stared at me as if he was trying to sort something out.

"Why? What's happened?" I asked.

"George got a call from Maria right before I left. He hung up and invited us to a fundraiser dinner. He wouldn't take no for an answer. No, it was more than that. It was the way he said it. It wasn't an invitation. It was more like a directive. I wonder what that's about."

"What kind of fundraiser?"

"For Manuel Antonio National Park. For conservation and preservation. Can you believe that?"

CHAPTER 12

Playa de Delfines, a private beach club a few miles north of the park, hosted the fundraiser. Tiki torches and glowing paper ball lanterns illuminated the beach and patio with a warm glow. A nice evening breeze carried the scent of salt. The surf unfurled unto the sand with a gentle, rhythmic gush that mixed with the easy Latin beat of the band. A temporary dance floor had been laid out on a deck where several couples swayed and twirled.

About two-hundred and fifty people were in attendance. Waiters in crisp white shirts casually moved about the crowd carrying trays of tropical drinks. A long table stretched the length of the patio, covered in white linens, its centerpiece a giant ice sculpture of a dolphin, and tray after tray of hors d'oeuvres— skewered shrimp, scallops wrapped in bacon, crackers covered in a dollop of ceviche, chorizo stuffed mushrooms. Nothing I'd eat. Once again, I'd be scrounging for a source of sustenance that didn't include animal flesh.

Dalton and I mingled, doing the only kind of intel gathering one can do at a party like this—see who's wearing what, or, in other words, who has money, who wants everyone to think they have money, basically who's maneuvering for power. You could easily identify the few couples who were actual donors. They sauntered about, arm in arm, gripping martinis, their lips permanently fixed with passive smiles.

I headed for a drink, but came to a halt. Isabella was behind the bar. I made a quick U-turn. If Isabella was working here tonight, that meant it was likely Carlos had his hand in this shindig somehow. I glanced around. There were several bars. At least I could avoid her.

I spotted Kevin, our new Australian friend, amid the crowd. Our eyes met and he immediately headed my way. I needed some information from him for my plan and was hoping to speak to him without Dalton overhearing, so I quickly closed the distance between us. "G'day, Ms. Brittany," he said. "Enjoyin' your visit?" The accent made me grin.

"Yes, it's a lovely country. The beach is gorgeous. I'm thinking of moving to a seaside room, maybe with a balcony. Our place is, well—" I curled my lip into an expression of dislike. "How about you? Do you like where you're staying?"

"Yeah, very nice little place to the north of here, the Casa del Mar. You should check it out."

"I will," I said with a wink. *Mission accomplished.*

Dalton appeared at my side.

"'Owdy, mate," Kevin said.

"Evenin'," Dalton said. They exchanged a manly that's-all-I-got nod. Charming conversationalists.

We stood in triangle formation for an uncomfortable moment before Kevin said, "Well, I's needing some grog. See yoos late-tah."

Dalton and I faced each other and casually scanned the crowd. Joe Nash was meandering our way, the cigar in his mouth. "There's Carl," I said to Dalton.

"John, right?" Nash said, offering his hand to Dalton as he approached.

Dalton nodded. "Nice to see you again."

"Likewise." He smiled at me. "John, my good man, mind if I take your lady for a spin around the dance floor?"

Dalton grinned. "Go right ahead." As I endured this old boy transaction I thought about my role and the plight of women everywhere, how women handle these situations with varying responses. Brittany would smile at Carl in a flirtatious way, enjoying the attention. Poppy would punch John in the nose and tell Carl to take a hike.

I flashed my Brittany smile and held out my hand to Nash.

Once we were on the dance floor, where the sound of our whispers would get lost in the music, he asked how things were going.

"Okay, I guess." I waited for a couple who seemed like they were hovering close by to pirouette in another direction before I added, "We've identified the kingpin." He raised an eyebrow. I whispered, "Maria."

"You're sure?"

I nodded. "Anything on your end?"

"Nothing that huge. But it gives me perspective."

I saw Dalton talking with Felix, the man from Germany. "Learn anything more about our foreign friends? I'm thinking the dinner was for her to assess potential buyers."

"It's a good theory. I'll see what I can find out."

The song was coming to an end. I wasn't sure how to ask Nash what I wanted to know, so I went ahead and said it. "Do you think she could also be running drugs?"

"Possible," he said. "Why? Any signs?"

I shook my head. "Just a hunch."

The song came to an end and I thanked him for the dance. "Be careful," he whispered in my ear before he sauntered toward the bar and I casually made my way through the crowd to Dalton and Felix. "Hello Felix," I said.

"Ah, Fräulein." He bowed in greeting, then pushed the greasy glasses up his nose. "How are you dis evening?"

"Very well, thank you." I wanted to find out, as quickly as I could, where he was staying, but he was going to be a tougher nut to crack than Kevin. "And you? What do you think of Costa Rica?"

"Zee veather is vonderful. Sun chine all day."

"Have you had time to walk on the beach?"

"Busy verking," he said, shaking his head.

I smiled and nodded like I was sympathizing. "Did you at least get a room with a view?"

"No, no."

I was getting nowhere.

The vibe in the party changed suddenly. All eyes turned toward the entrance where Maria strode in, George a couple paces behind her, which I'm sure was by directive. Of course, they were fashionably late, which was right on time for a grand entrance.

Maria demanded attention in a tight-fitting red bandeau dress, her girls pressed together and showing eight miles of cleavage, the skirt knee length, slit up the side to her waist with a black ruffled edge. As if that wasn't flashy enough, she wore purple and red sparkly earrings and wrist bangles. To top if off, she glided across the floor on red velvet pumps sporting four-inch heels.

I had on a cornflower blue sundress, cotton, sleeveless. Nice, cool and comfortable. I whispered to Dalton. "Do you find that attractive?"

"Um," he didn't take his eyes from her. "No comment?"

I almost sprained my eye socket doing an eye roll.

George and Maria worked the crowd before making their way to us. They thanked us for coming, for all the support, blah, blah. What a load of crap. Dalton and I smiled and nodded and acted the part as I tried to figure out why she wanted us here. Certainly to appear as though she had clout, as though she had the ear of big donors. Money and influence drove Maria, that was obvious. But why us?

She and George hobnobbed their way to the podium which had been placed at the side of the dance floor. A man in a white suit coat stepped to the microphone and hushed the crowd. Must have been the head of the nonprofit for which this fundraiser was hosted. After a rather boring overview, he launched into a glowing introduction of Maria Mendoza Hillman.

She strutted to the podium, taking her time while all the eyes were on her. "Good evening," she said in her perfect English. "Tonight is a celebration of all that is good and beautiful in Costa Rica. I don't have to tell you how vital it is that we keep it that way. Our heritage, the mighty rainforest, is at risk."

The crowd made a collective nod of agreement. I squeezed Dalton's hand and glared at Maria. *You lying hypocrite.*

"We must, all of us, do our part to support this organization and their good works. *Mis amigos*, please, open your pocketbooks."

My teeth had a firm grasp on my tongue. *Indeed, for if there is no rainforest, there are no animals to steal.*

"Together, we can keep our country lush and green."

Applause. I forced my hands together. Thankfully her speech was short and to the point. I don't think I could have stomached any more.

The band started up again in a hot, latino salsa beat, the volume cranked up two-fold. George and Maria took to the dance floor. I watched as they and other couples shook and bounced and twirled.

Dalton, standing next to me, said, "The trick is to swing your hips."

My head snapped in his direction. "You dance?"

He shrugged. "I like holding a lady in my arms. If I have to move my feet to do it, well, I know a few steps."

The tune changed to a slow waltz. He downed the rest of his beer, set the bottle on a tray, and held out his hand. "Shall we?"

I wouldn't call myself a great dancer, but I do all right with a strong lead. When I was a child, no matter where we happened to be in the world, my father would find an American oldies music station on the radio and I'd stand on the top of his feet and he would twirl me around the room. He taught me the fox trot, the mamba, the waltz, the rhumba, the cha cha cha. I haven't had another dance partner since and I was feeling a bit rusty.

Dalton led me to the dance floor, then turned to face me, his left hand held out to the side for me to take. "It's like sex," he said as he placed his right hand on the small of my back and pulled me tightly to him. "Move your hips with mine." He waggled his eyebrows. "On the beat, step back with your right foot. I'll take it from there."

I counted—one-two-three, one-two-three—then stepped back and we were in motion, moving as one, my body so close to his, it felt fluid, natural. I twirled, spinning round the axis that was Dalton as he led me around the floor. I didn't think about the steps, about the rhythm, it just was. Being in his arms was easy, letting him take control. He moved and I moved with him.

By the end of the song, I was breathless. He held my hand tightly and eased me backward into a dip. When he pulled me upward, I stopped inches from his lips, his hot breath on my face. He leaned forward and kissed me ever so gently. I was glad to have his arms around me because I thought I might melt.

Who said I couldn't look like the wife, hopelessly in love? *We've got this nailed.*

My hand held high in the air like a professional dancer, he twirled me around and led me off the dance floor into the crowd, where we ran smack into Noah.

For a moment, his presence didn't jive in my brain. What was he doing here? In a tux? My mouth opened to speak, but I couldn't. I couldn't acknowledge him at all. I'd blow my cover. But there was nothing stopping him from blowing it for me. Right now. *Please, Noah. Don't say anything. Please.*

He stared at me with an unreadable expression, then his eyes zoomed in on my hand and the diamond I wore. They refocused to assess Dalton, then shifted back to me. There was more than disappointment in his eyes; there was something that looked more like condemnation, as though he'd received an answer to a question he'd been purposely avoiding. My heart sank.

For a moment, I thought he might turn away, before anyone noticed, but his eyes were locked on Dalton. Noah offered his hand to Dalton. "You must be Brittany's...husband?"

Crap. Isn't there some unspoken code about affairs? You don't purposefully meet the husband.

Dalton quickly looked to me for an explanation.

"John, dear, I met this nice gentleman at the butterfly garden. You remember. I told you I had stopped by."

Dalton's hand squeezed mine. This was a problem. I needed to do something. Now.

I steeled myself. "This really isn't a good time," I said with emphasis, willing him to take the hint. "Perhaps we can discuss our donation to your cause another time." My eyes locked with his. *Please, just go with it, Noah. Walk away.*

Noah eyed Dalton, assessing him. His eyes shifted back to me and held for a long moment. *Please, Noah. Take the hint.*

He held up his hands and backed away.

"Forgive me," I said.

My words hung in the air as Noah disappeared in the crowd.

I turned and caught sight of Maria, staring at me through the crowd.

"Let's get a drink," I said and steered Dalton toward the bar.

We were steps away when Maria materialized out of nowhere. "Where have you been hiding?" she said to Dalton, a wicked grin on her face. I opened my mouth to speak but she had him by the arm. "I've been hoping for a dance."

I watched as she led him to the dance floor and pressed her body against his. He twirled her around while she shook her fanny and made an ass of herself. What was she thinking? Like he'd go for a gold-digger like her. *Wait, what do I care? I don't like him in that way. Sure he's hot but.... But he's* my *husband.*

When the song finally ended, he gave her a polite thank you

and what looked like goodbyes for the evening. He took me by the arm and practically dragged me out the door and into the car.

"What's going on?"

Dalton kept his gaze forward, his eyes on the road. "She knows something. I've been doing this a long time. I can tell. She's suspicious."

"Why? What did she say?"

"That kid,"—*kid?*—"you said he knew about her operation, that he had some evidence? What does he know?"

"I—" *Crap.* "I'm not sure. You told me not to talk to him again."

He glared at me. "And since you've been here, you've followed my every order?"

I frowned. "Is that steam coming out of your ears?"

We headed into the downtown area. "You need to fix this. Make sure this situation is neutralized."

"Neutralized? What the hell are you suggesting?"

He pulled the car to the curb at a busy block in town. "Go talk to him. Find out if she knows who he is. We need to get a handle on this."

"Right now? The butterfly garden isn't open at this hour. How do you expect—"

"You're going to lie to me now?"

I stared into those eyes. Those beautiful eyes. The same eyes that looked at me with loving sympathy when I'd sobbed into his shirt. "No, I'm not." I got out of the car. He drove away before the door was shut.

Chapter 13

The lights were on in the tree house and I could hear the slow, melancholy sound of a Joni Mitchell tune on the guitar. I ascended the staircase and sat down in one of the rattan chairs. Noah strummed his guitar without looking up, made no acknowledgement of my presence. I waited till the end of the song.

His eyes turned on me. "So are you a cop or something?" His words were laced with sarcasm and thrown at me with the same inflection as I had asked him that first day. He reached for his bottle of beer and tipped it up. I watched his movement for any sign of his intentions.

"Fish and Wildlife," I finally said.

"I suppose that guy's your partner then?"

"Yes. We are undercover as a married couple."

His lip curled up in a sarcastic grin. "Yeah, I figured."

"All right," I said, half relieved, half annoyed. "How'd you figure?"

"Well, for starters, when you first arrived at the butterfly garden, you were wearing a wedding ring." He exaggerated a nod. "Yep, first thing I noticed. Then it was gone. But there was something about you. I just couldn't make you for a player. Too…"

"Young and innocent?"

"Something like that." His eyes traveled down my body

and back up again. "Then your kung fu moves on the guard up there in the hills. And c'mon. Got lost birding?" He rolled out of the hammock, pushed a stack of magazines to one side of the coffee table, and sat down on the edge facing me. He reached up and ran a finger through my hair. "This is fiery red, not dumb blond."

"All circumstantial," I said. I couldn't tell if he was mad and toying with me, or amused and flirting with me. Either way, I was totally turned on.

"Ah, but the true tip off, the crème de la crème, the icing on the cake, the—"

"All right already."

"Only feds call the middleman the buncher."

I closed my eyes. "Damn."

His hand caressed my cheek. "It was so adorable."

I suck at this.

"I didn't realize you weren't working alone."

"Yeah, about that—"

"You and your husband—" he leaned in and kissed me on my neck, just below my ear "—looked awfully into each other on the dance floor."

My breath caught in my throat. "It's my job. That's my cover."

He moved farther down my neck.

I shook my head. "I thought you'd be angry with me."

"Angry?" He pulled back and looked into my eyes. "I don't know if I can keep my hands off you."

I smiled, relieved. I cocked my head to the side and matched his intensity with my gaze. "While we're being honest, what's your story?"

He sat back. "What do you mean?"

"I think you want your friends to believe you're a trust funder, but I don't buy it."

He flashed an innocent smile.

"At first glance, this is a modest tree house. But ocean front property? I bet you own it. You're not Isabella's neighbor, you're her landlord."

He kept his expression the same, but I saw the slightest flinch of acknowledgement.

"And the Chateau Montelena Estate Cabernet Sauvignon—nice taste by the way—that wine retails for nearly two-hundred dollars. Trust funders don't spend that kind of coin on wine. They go to Europe, ski the Alps. You earned your money."

He wouldn't nod, but I knew I was right. I placed my hand on his thigh and slid it forward as I leaned in. "But the true reveal, the final blow, the…" I paused. "Damn, I can't think of another idiom."

He grinned and shook his head. "Go on."

"Financial lingo. Hedging? Selling futures? My bet is Yale, left before you even graduated to take on Wall Street. Am I close?"

He ran his fingers through my hair. "I knew you were a natural red." He held my head in his hand, gently pulled me toward him, and nuzzled the soft spot right above my collarbone, then worked his way up my neck, leaving a trail of kisses that made me shiver with desire.

He pulled away from me again, leaving me breathless, his hazel eyes mischievously assessing me. "So we know each other's deepest secrets." He grinned. "Now what do we do?"

"Anything we want," I said and practically launched out of the chair into his arms, hungry for his lips on me, his tongue. I tugged at his T-shirt and yanked it over his head.

He wrapped his arms around me and spun us around. He surprised me with his strength; he held me with his left arm as he knocked the magazines to the floor. He lay me down on my back on the coffee table and slowly crawled on top of me, taking his time to enjoy the curves of my body, working his way back up to my neck. He buried his head in my hair and whispered in my ear, "God, you're hot."

I grabbed onto him, shifted to my hip, and rolled to straddle him. The table tipped and we fell to the floor with a thump, me sprawled on top of him. The table slammed to the floor with a bang. "I'm sorry. I'm sorry," I said. I pushed myself up on my hands but kept my body pressed against him.

He laughed, rubbing the back of his head. "Wow, you are feisty."

I had nothing to lose. "Yes, I am." I ran my hands down his chest to the button on his jeans.

He shoved the table out of the way. "Let's wreck this place."

I lay in his arms. "I'm sorry I lied to you," I said. "I had to. It's my job. Even though, obviously," I sighed, "I'm not very good at it." I shifted so I could see his eyes. "But it was for the greater good."

"Most honorable." He kissed the tip of my nose. "And you are good at it. I'm just really good at reading people." He gently stroked my hair. "I used to swindle people for a living."

"What? I don't believe that."

"Even if it was legal, that's what I did." He pushed himself up on the pillow. "But I wasn't always like that."

I propped myself up on my elbow. "I bet I know one thing for sure; you've always liked insects."

His grin was laced with nostalgia. "When I was a kid, I loved bugs. My Uncle Frank got me this really cool ant farm for Christmas one year. I'd watch them for hours. Fascinating, you know, how industrious they are. My father hated it, of course. Said it was a waste of time.

"One day, he was angry because I didn't have my homework finished or something, I don't remember. He was always mad at me for something. Anyway, I'll never forget how he stomped around my room in a rage and knocked it off my dresser. I swear it hovered in mid air, you know that defining moment, and I was helpless to stop it." He winced at the memory. "It was like time froze, just so I'd have to endure that agony. Then it smashed on the floor and shattered. Sand and dirt flew everywhere. The ants skittered around in circles. They didn't know which way to go. Their entire world had been destroyed in an instant, shattered to bits. My father stomped his foot right in the center of it, smooshing them to death."

"He made it clear. Nothing else mattered but perfect grades. I was going to business school. It wasn't an option. He didn't care whether that's what I wanted to do. My dream of being an entomologist was pointless to him. I couldn't have hobbies, play sports. Nothing that wasn't an *approved* extracurricular activity." His eyes traveled down my chest. "Girls were most definitely off limits."

He paused as though he wasn't sure he wanted to tell me any more of the story. He turned to look me in the eyes. "Yes, I went to Yale. Got a job in the secondary mortgage market. I was exactly what my father wanted me to be." He shook his head with disgust. "I was a selfish sonofabitch. I wanted to make money. Lots of it. And I did."

"What happened? What changed?"

"One day, this guy Mark, asked me to go for a walk. We were friends, I guess. As good of friends as two guys in finance can be. He wanted to get out of the office, tell me about an opportunity he didn't want overheard. Funny part about it was, I'd just bought this new suit, custom tailored. Three grand. Mark shows up in the same suit and gives me crap about finding my own style.

"Anyway, we walked to the corner of the block. There was this tiny park there, you know, a patch of grass, one tree and a bench. He was telling me about this company that was over leveraged, how he could take over, liquidate, some mom and pop outfit that held a patent of which they didn't realize the value. We got to the bench and there was a homeless man sitting there feeding the pigeons. Everything he owned in the world was in the bag on the ground next to him, but he was sharing what he had with the pigeons. I don't know why. The joy of their companionship maybe, maybe to feel like he was helping."

His eyes turned glassy with the memory. I didn't want to interrupt his story. So I waited.

"Mark wanted to sit on the bench, but he wasn't going to sit down next to some stinking homeless man—his words—so he walked up to him and told him to move along, get a job. The man didn't flinch, didn't acknowledge Mark."

He paused again. Closed his eyes.

"What'd Mark do?" I asked.

"He kicked a pigeon. Sent it flying into the tree trunk. It flopped around on the ground, its wing broken. The old man looked up at Mark. There was no fear in his eyes. Just pity. Pity for Mark." He clenched his teeth together and I was sure it was to hold back a tear. "The old man got up. Mark thought it was because he'd intimidated him into leaving. Mark plopped down in the seat without a second thought and starting talking strategy, about a partnership." He shook his head. "The old man shuffled over to the base of the tree and drove the heel of his boot down on the bird, putting it out of its misery. Then he poked around in his bag and pulled out a spoon and right next to where Mark sat, the old man dug a grave for that bird."

"Wow, that's…" I didn't know what to say.

"And I sat there next to him. In the same damn suit."

I gave him a moment before I asked, "What'd you do?"

"I went back to the office, packed up my things, and walked out. I've never been back." He shifted and met my eyes. "I like it much better here. Don't you agree?"

"Yeah," I said and as if he'd been cued, Clyde bounded up the side of the balcony. "You're in good company."

Noah got up and tossed a biscuit to Clyde. While the little visitor crunched away at it, Noah adjusted the pillows we'd piled up on the floor beneath us and eased back into place, his arms around me. "What made you want to be a wildlife cop?"

"Hold on. You don't just volunteer at the butterfly garden, do you?"

He grinned. "Don't go changing the subject. I asked *you* a question."

"Fine." I thought of my dad, but I couldn't go there. Not right now. "I can't stand to see animals being hurt. And I love being outdoors. I can't imagine a job in a city, in a cubicle somewhere. It'd be the death of me."

"No kidding. Tell me about it."

"I just don't understand how anyone can hurt an animal the way these criminals do and think nothing of it. The horror, the tragedy of it all. It's mind-boggling. I always wondered how these people can be so heartless. I'm starting to see it's more about the human capacity for denial. That combined with plain ignorance. I mean, anyone who's ever had a dog ought to see that animals have feelings. They feel pain." Clyde finished his biscuit and bounded across the room and jumped up and down at our feet.

"Did you clean up the crumbs?" Noah said.

Clyde scurried back and swept the floor with his tiny hand.

"I'll get it," I said and got up for another biscuit. I held it in my hand, wanting Clyde to take it from me. He approached without hesitation, his high-pitched whine as cute as can be. "See, he knows. Instinctively or otherwise, he knows I'm a friend. He's smarter than we are in some ways." I clenched my jaw, anger stirring in me. "But humans have the immense capacity to be deceitful. We have better traps, better weapons, better cages."

Noah sat up. "So you're a fed. What are you doing here in Costa Rica?"

"Not nearly enough," I said. "But you can help."

"Tell me how."

"Does Maria know you're the one who has been targeting her operation?"

"I don't know how she would."

"Would she recognize you for any other reason? Does she know you're an activist?"

He kinda half shook his head. "She might. If she went out of her way to investigate."

I nodded. She certainly would have done that. "I have an idea."

"Will it save animals?"

I smiled wide. "We could use the gang, too."

"Tell me when."

"Tomorrow morning, I'll be back. We'll plan our attack."

I had all day. After I'd assured Dalton that Maria couldn't possibly know Noah, not to worry, he left for his morning five-mile run and after that he'd planned a day of sorting through snakes and frogs, then going to play cards again, so he'd probably be late.

I stopped at the Coco-Cabana, dragged Chris out of his bed, and we headed for the tree house.

"Noah, this is Chris. He's a friend. Not a cop."

Noah shook Chris's hand. "Coffee's almost ready," he said and tromped across the rope bridge.

Chris raised an eyebrow at me and mouthed the word *wow*.

"He's straight," I whispered.

He raised the other eyebrow.

I grinned. "Very straight."

Clyde bounded up the stairs, Isabella not far behind him. "Buenos días," I said.

"Buenos días," she groaned, one eye open.

"Noah's coming with coffee," I told her, which caused a slight uptick in her step.

Chris and Clyde were making fast friends. Chris held his arm out and Clyde swung on it like a trapeze artist. "He's so cute," Chris cooed.

Jack and Doug arrived, Jack with a bag of doughnuts and

Doug carrying a watermelon. Noah came across the bridge with a pot of coffee and three mugs in his hands. "Grab some more mugs," he said to Jack. "And let's take this to the picnic table. This old tree house is pretty sturdy"—he winked at me—"but I'm not sure how many people it'll hold."

Matt and Claudia walked up as we plopped everything on the picnic table. "Amanda and Colette will be here soon. Dan and Sierra have to work."

The morning sun felt warm on my back. I dug my bare toes into the sand.

Their hands wrapped around warm mugs of coffee, the others sat down forming a circle around me. "This is going to be dangerous," I said. "If you don't want to be involved, I understand. Just say so now." They each looked around at the others, none of them wanting to bow out. "All right." I assessed my team, then turned to Chris, Jack, and Doug. "My plan is a bit, well, bold." I grinned. "I think its time Maria had a little competition. Chris, meet Doug and Jack, your bodyguards."

"What do I need bodyguards for?"

"You're a wildlife smuggler. A very successful one. And you're moving in on the competition."

Doug piped up. "I'm not trained for that sort of thing."

"You're an actor, right? It's all for show." He nodded, the concept slowly settling in.

"Your first task: go shopping."

Chris gave me his yeah-I'm-gay-but-c'mon look. "Seriously?"

"You need to dress for success." I turned to Doug and Jack. "You, too. Ex-military, green beret types. Can you do that?"

They nodded, excited.

I turned to the rest of the group. "They'll need a car."

Noah jumped to his feet. "This way." We all followed him into the trees to a structure built with corrugated tin panels. He lifted the latch on a sliding door and pushed it open. "This work?" Parked inside was a shiny new black SUV.

"Perfect."

Doug slapped him on the back. "You've been holding out on us, man."

"Nice ride, dude," said Jack.

Noah turned to Doug. "You drive."

"We'll need the VW, too," I said.

Noah shrugged. "Whatever."

As we walked back to the beach together, I explained that we'd be visiting some potential buyers. Chris asked, "How will we convince them to leave Maria and buy from me?"

"Oh, we don't have to convince them of anything. We go talk to them, about the weather, whatever. As long as we're seen doing it."

"But what if she asks?"

"She won't. But if she does, even better. They'll say we talked about the weather, because we did. Of course, she'll think they're lying."

"But I don't see what that does if there isn't a real threat," said Jack.

"The threat doesn't have to be real. She only has to think that it's real."

We sat back down in the sand. Noah said, "This whole plan depends on your judgement of Maria. That she has people watching, that she'll act on this. You're giving her a lot of credit."

"She didn't get to be a world-class wildlife trafficker by being stupid." I looked him in the eye. "And she's not going to let it go very easily either. That's our advantage. We know her goal and we know what she's afraid of. The key is to guide her in the direction we want her to go, without her realizing it. We do what fortunetellers do. We give her the right bits of information and let her connect the dots."

He shook his head. I wasn't sure if he was skeptical or in awe of my great insight.

I turned to Isabella. She likely had the best information I

needed for the other part of my plan. "Have you ever seen Maria come to The Toucan to see Carlos? The woman from the fundraiser?"

Isabella shook her head.

"Okay, just tell me what you know about Carlos, everything you know."

She made a disgusted face. "I don like heem."

Noah answered. "He owns The Toucan, a hangout for tourists who get off the cruise ships, mostly a lunch crowd. All regular deliveries, the food, alcohol, come in the morning, like any other bar. But it's a front for the smuggling. During the lunch rush, when the place is too busy for anyone to notice, locals show up, delivering boxes to the storeroom, a shed out back, behind the kitchen."

"Everyday, the same time?" I asked.

"During lunch. We figure they're the poachers. Carlos hangs out back with his right hand man. Whenever a poacher arrives with something to sell, he sends his man into the bar to get cash from the till."

"How big is the shed? Big enough to house these animals?"

He shook his head. "They load them right into the panel truck. Carlos just hangs out back there, smoking all day. At two-thirty, Paco drives away in the van and Carlos empties the till and leaves in his own car."

I turned to Isabella. "What about drugs? He running those through the bar?"

"I don know," she said. "I never seen no drugs."

"So it's possible they are in one of these mystery boxes, then?"

Noah said, "We didn't know there were drugs until you and I—"

"Right, got it," I said. Everyone didn't need to know about our escapade. "So if there are drugs, they'd be in the panel van, headed to wherever the animals are taken."

Jack piped up. "We rode the van once. To the shed at the old coffee plantation. That's how we knew about it."

"All right, what about—wait, what do you mean you rode the van?"

Jack grinned. "We roof surfed. You know, like hood surfing, only on the roof." He put out his hands like he was balancing on a surf board.

"You're kidding right?"

He stared at me, his brow knit. Like why wouldn't that be possible?

Amanda and Colette came walking down the beach, hand in hand. They filled coffee cups and joined us. "What's going on?" Colette asked.

Doug held up his mug. "We're going to kick some wildlife smuggler ass!" he said.

I thanked them for coming, but my head was still at The Toucan. "Does the van go to the shed at the plantation everyday? Or could there be multiple locations?"

Noah shrugged. He looked to Jack and Doug. They shrugged. Noah said, "We do know that the van comes back in the evening. They drive down on the dock. Everyday by five. That's when the shipments go out. Then the empty van gets parked behind The Toucan for the next day."

"All right." To Amanda and Colette, I said. "You two can impersonate drunk college girls, right? You have bikinis?" They nodded. "And Amanda, I have a computer question. We can chat about that in a bit. What we need to know right away is details about the whereabouts of the drugs. We need to know what day they ship. I need surveillance on the shed at the plantation." I looked at Noah. "It's not a fun job, but I can't be seen with you. Will you do it?"

He nodded and turned to Matt and Claudia, the river guides. "I'll need your help."

"Anything," they said simultaneously.

"Make sure you have enough supplies to camp out up there for a couple days if need be," I said. "Take your cell phones.

Make sure they're charged and keep them off until you need to contact me. There's no cell coverage up there. You'll need to hike out a ways to get service. So as soon as you see the van—wait a minute." I turned to Isabella. "Did you say Paco? Is there more than one Paco?"

"I don know."

Could it be? Could I be that lucky? Agent García had likely chosen Paco because it was such a common name but—"How long has Paco been with Carlos?"

Isabella shook her head. Noah, too. Isabella said, "This Paco, I haf seen him around, but only a few month does he get dee money and drive dee ban."

"Do you work today?"

"Sí, everyday at eleven."

To Chris, Jack, and Doug, I said, "Get shopping. Be dressed and in character and meet me at The Toucan at noon. Get a table close to an exit."

Chapter 14

I had to change my clothes, grab a few things, and, this time, make sure Yipes followed me to where I was going for lunch. I popped into the bungalow and ran into Dalton.

"There you are," he said. "I thought you were going up to the cocina for some coffee and you'd be right back."

"I went for a walk. What are you doing here? I thought you had frogs to sort."

"I'm taking the day off. Gonna spend it with you like we had planned for yesterday. I was just going to call you."

Crap. I had to get back to The Toucan. This would blow everything. I had to think. Fast. I smirked. "Yeah, you don't need to babysit me. I'm behaving." I made sure he heard the sarcasm and disappointment in my voice. "It's already getting hot out there. Thought I'd change and go shopping. Yay!" I snatched my khaki shorts and a tank top from my suitcase, waltzed into the bathroom, and shut the door.

I quickly changed, trying to think of what else I might need so I could grab it and go. I opened the door and Dalton was standing right there, blocking my way.

"I want you to know," he said, his jaw muscles tight, "that I'm sorry. I've been on your case since you got here. I haven't given you a fair chance." His eyes dropped to his hands. He examined his cuticles, then the backs of his hands. Finally his eyes came back to mine. "You were right. I screwed up and that's why they

sent you down here and, well, I was ticked off."

"I understand," I said. "Don't worry about it." I pushed by him and headed for the door. He grabbed me by the arm and spun me around.

"Wait, that's it?" He looked hurt. "I'm trying to tell you I'm sorry." He threw up his hands. "God, women!"

I screwed my face into a smile. "I'm just saying, no apology needed. I get it. This op is important to you and you don't want anything to jeopardize it. I respect that."

"Thank you," he said. He actually looked relieved. God he was such a sweet guy. *Dammit. My plan better work.* He took my hand in his. "I'm actually glad you're here. The way you figured out it was Maria so quickly."

I blushed a little.

"I was thinking maybe…"

"Yeah, no." I yanked my hand away. "We've got a job to do here." I gave him a stern look. I had to be stern.

"Wow, you really don't like compliments, do you?"

"Do you compliment Joe?" I had to pick a fight.

"What?" He stepped back. "Why would I?"

"I bet you wouldn't spend the day at the beach with him. So you could *finally see him in a bikini.*" The last words I spat at him, dripping with sarcasm. "I get it. I'm here on your turf. But you also made it abundantly clear who's in charge. This job's important to me too and I'm doing exactly as you told me. Shopping, going to the beach. Staying the hell out of your way. I'm being the good, obedient wife. You don't have to rub it in." And I was out the door, feeling like a heel.

When I got to The Toucan, the guys were already there, halfway through three baskets of fish fingers and a bucket of Cerveza Imperials. I had to take my time getting there to make sure Yipes could follow. I sat down at the table with them. My eyes on Chris, I said to Jack and Doug, "Remember, boys, don't talk to me. You're the muscle. My business is with Chris." They didn't flinch. Excellent. "We're going to chat. You look confident, comfortable. I'll shift in my seat a few times."

Chris nodded. Acted nonchalant, in control. He was good at this.

"Now, sit tight," I said. "And easy on the beer." I went to the bar and waved Isabella over. "Next time Paco comes in, point me out to him and tell him I'm also hunting a beautiful butterfly and that he looks like he could use a bathroom break."

She looked at me with a quizzical expression.

"Make sure you say exactly that."

"Okay," she said with a shrug and went back to work.

I leaned on the bar and waited, trying to blend in with the tourists. Finally, a man slipped behind the counter and went straight for the cash register. Isabella was so busy she didn't notice him. I got her attention and motioned in his direction with my eyes. She spun around and caught him by the sleeve as he was headed back out. She whispered to him and he looked right at me. *This better be him. Otherwise, this whole plan disintegrates fast.* He listened to her, his eyes on me, then with the slightest nod, he left. Isabella brought me an IPA and said with a shrug, "I toll heem."

"Thanks."

I moved through the crowd and around to the outside corner to the restrooms. I waited until the area was clear and slipped into the men's room.

Men's rooms, I've found, are a microcosm of life. When left to their own devices, men are simply pigs. God knows when the last time this place was cleaned. Paper towels were strewn on the floor, soap dispenser missing altogether. I slipped into a stall, prepared to stand on the toilet seat if necessary, but hoped it didn't come to that.

I didn't have to wait long. The door eased open and I heard it close and the click of the lock.

I slipped from the stall. "I'm a friend of Joe's." I watched his reaction. "Joe Nash."

"I don't know nobody name'a Joe." He wasn't going to blow his cover no matter what. He walked to the stall, looked inside, walked back and grabbed me by the arm and slammed me against the wall. He ran his hands up my right leg, then my left. He spun me around and checked under my arms.

"Who the hell are you?" he said.

"Martin showed me the postcard."

"What do you want?" He frowned. "And this better be good. Make it quick."

"Carlos running coke?"

"I think so. But on the side. Definitely not sanctioned by his boss."

I crossed my arms. "You think so or you know so?"

He shook his head. "Whenever we get a poisonous snake, Carlos takes the afternoon delivery on his own. I just figured. Only thing that makes sense."

"Right," I said. Drug dealers were known to use aggressive or venomous animals to guard their inventory. He probably hid the drugs in a secret compartment in the bottom of a crate. Snake on top. Border agents aren't likely to mess with it and the fine is minor for the snake. "Any particular day?"

"No. But we got one this morning, if that helps."

That didn't give me much time.

He crossed his arms. "Directive from Virginia is to stay the course."

"Right," I said. "We're just working another angle. What else can you tell me?"

"Not much really. These guys are amateurs." He glanced toward the door. "Amateurs with guns. I'm gone too long, I'm toast."

"I've got it covered. At the far table, three guys. Smuggler and his bodyguards. The competition. Make it be known you've just been solicited and turned him down. Solidify your loyalty, help our cause."

He pondered this a moment, then nodded slowly. "I gotta go." He moved toward the door.

"One more thing," I said. "How'd you know it was Maria?"

"Who?"

"On the postcard, you said you had your sights set on a butterfly."

"I always hear him on the phone. I figured it was a woman in charge because he calls her Mariposa. That's all I know. I was hoping Nash could connect the dots."

"It's his sister, Maria. She's the kingpin."

He nodded as if this made sense. "Good. We're getting closer. I'm getting tired of this asshole." He slid out the door, looked both ways, and nodded to me that it was clear.

I went straight to the table. "Carlos will be looking out here at you any minute now. Make sure he sees you, then get the hell out of here fast," I said and melted into the crowd where I could keep an eye on them.

Chris hailed the waitress. When she dropped the check on the table, he slapped her on the ass. I did an eye roll. He was getting cocky already. He looked up and hesitated. He whispered to Doug. He seemed to have caught sight of something. I spun around. Carlos and two thugs were headed toward him. *Oh no.* I moved closer.

"¿Qué te lleva a mi bar?" Carlos asked.

Crap! Chris doesn't speak Spanish.

Chris sat back in his chair, interlaced his fingers, and casually looked up at Carlos. "Nice place," he said. "The beer was cold—" he flicked his finger at the baskets on the table "—but the grouper was a bit soggy."

"What do you want?"

Chris grinned, his eyes traveled to a waitress who was bending over, wiping the table nearby. "Just enjoying the view."

Carlos shifted on his feet. "Well I suggest you find another one. Move on down the beach."

Chris slowly surveyed the scene, peering out at the water,

the beach, the cruise ship at the dock, the cargo ships docked along the pier. "I don't know." He turned back to Carlos and grinned. "I kinda like it here. You know what they say: location, location, location."

God, Chris, don't push it.

Carlos crossed his arms, his neck muscles pulled taut. His thugs moved in.

Chris pushed back his chair and rose to his feet. Doug and Jack rose on either side of him. Chris adjusted his shirt collar, then brushed down the front of his silk shirt, smoothing it out real nice. He made a show of looking around the bar, up at the rafters, from corner to corner as he pulled his sleeves at the cuffs. Then he winked at Carlos. "Yeah, I like it here a lot." He turned to Doug. "Shall we?" And he strolled out like he owned the place.

"That was awesome!" said Doug. He was at the wheel and we were speeding down the main road.

"Holy crap, Chris," I said. "That was risky. That could've gone south, fast."

He grinned at me. "Yeah, but it didn't."

Jack gave him a shove on the shoulder. "Dude, you're crazy. All I could think was how I was going to learn kung ku, like if I could get an instant download like in The Matrix. Dude, that was messed up."

"Where to next, boss?" Doug asked.

Chris pointed at me. "You'll have to ask her."

I gave him a head slap. "He meant me." To Doug I said, "Casa del Mar, a little hotel on the beach, north of the Playa de Delfines resort."

"I know it," he said. "What's the plan there? We going to rough up some poachers?"

"No!" I glared at him even though he couldn't see me with his eyes on the road. "Chris and I are going in to talk to someone.

You and Jack hang out at the door, looking around like Secret Service. Make yourselves obvious. But not too obvious. Know what I mean?"

"Sure, boss," Doug said.

"You don't have to call me boss."

"Hey, I'm a method actor. I'm getting into my role. Just go with it."

I rubbed my temples with my thumb and middle finger. Maybe this wasn't such a good idea, I thought. It made me think of Roy. And the Lawson brothers. I bet he enjoyed nailing their partner.

I texted Amanda and Colette to let them know to be ready, today was the day.

Then my phone rang. It was Claudia. "Dead!" she burst. "They killed a man. Killed him!"

"Take a breath. Tell me exactly what happened."

The connection was staticky. "They came on horses like you said, Maria and a man. They went into the shed. Then we heard gunshots. She left with the horses and—" Claudia whimpered "—the guards dragged the man's body out into the jungle."

"Noah and Matt are okay?"

"Yes," she said.

"All right. What did the man look like? Anything you remember about him?"

"He wore glasses. These ugly, old glasses, like from the seventies."

Felix. The German buyer. What had he done? "Okay, listen to me. This will be over soon. Everything's going to happen today. Tell Noah to mark the van somehow before it leaves. We need to know for sure we have the right van. Do you understand? We only have one shot at this."

"Okay, but I had to hike out to get cell service. I've got to hike back up there."

"As fast as you can. And be careful," I said then disconnected.

So Maria killed Felix. I felt a hole open in the pit of my stomach. I knew she was dangerous, but… Should I tell Dalton and Nash? No. Then I'd have to explain how I knew. I wondered what he had done. Didn't matter. I had to go on with the plan.

We pulled into the lot and I pushed it from my mind.

The Casa del Mar was a quaint little seaside motel with purple walls strangled by tropical foliage. I went into the office and asked for Kevin—*crap, I don't know his last name*. The staffer behind the desk was a sweet young gal with a cherub face, her long straight hair pulled back and pinned with wood barrettes. I leaned toward her and said in a whisper, "Australian guy. Very yummy." I tried to blush. The hardest thing to fake. "He, uh, left something in my room last night and I, uh, think he probably needs it back right away."

She nodded, enjoying the gossip fodder. "Room seven," she said. "But I think I just saw him out by the pool."

I winked and slipped out, Chris behind me.

We headed for the beach side and the pool area—me, Chris and his bodyguards. I rounded the corner and caught sight of Kevin, sprawled out on a lounge chair in his swimming trunks, a fruity drink in his hand. I told Chris to tell Doug and Jack to hang back and I walked up to Kevin and halted at his feet. He recognized me right away, I could tell, but he scanned behind me, quickly to my left, then my right. His eyes came to a screeching halt when he spotted Doug and Jack. "Miss Brittany," he said, sitting up on the edge of his chair. "To what do I owe the pleasha?"

"It's nice to see you," I said with a big smile. "This is my friend, Chris."

Chris acknowledged him with a curt nod.

"'Owdy, mate," Kevin said. I could tell he was running through scenarios in his mind, possible reasons I was here.

"Actually, I feel silly now that I'm standing here." I had planned on the bodyguards hanging outside his door, not having to explain them to him.

"Naw, it's awright." He leapt to his feet and grabbed the lounge chair nearby, spun it around, and offered for me to sit as he eased back into his chair.

"Thanks," I said. "But we don't need to stay and bother you." I quickly scanned the pool area. A waiter on the far side was lingering over a table, looking our way. Shazam. Kevin had his own Yipes. That meant he wasn't in with Maria and I'd accomplished my goal.

"Oh, you're no botha," Kevin said, smiling, his brow knit. I had him baffled. "No botha at-tall."

"Where are my manners? Here you are, relaxing by the pool, and we barge right in. It can wait until later." I nudged Chris. "We should go."

Kevin got to his feet. The gentleman. "No need."

"Maybe we could schedule a lunch?"

"What's this all about?"

"Oh, just a silly idea I had. Really, it's nothing." All I needed now was for him to nod. A reluctant nod. "So, lunch tomorrow then?"

He smiled. And then the nod. *Thank you, Kevin!*

As we headed back to the SUV, Chris whispered to me, "The pecs on that guy. And the accent. Oooooh. My god, girl, no wonder you're coming apart at the seams."

CHAPTER 15

We dropped Chris off at the Coco-Cabana. I told him to get packed and head straight to the airport. "But I could still—"

"No argument, Chris. You were a big help. I couldn't have done this without you. But it's too dangerous. Tell me you'll go right now. Get on the next flight out."

He nodded grudgingly. "You be careful, too," he said.

I checked my watch. It was four thirty-five. "I'll call you as soon as I get back in the States. I promise." I gave him a hug. "Thank you."

"Just get the bastards," he said with a grin.

I hopped in the SUV and slammed the door. "Get back to The Toucan. Now!"

In the short time Doug had been in Costa Rica, he had learned to drive like a tico. He weaved in and out of the lanes, passing on a double yellow line, up a blind hill. No problem. "Good way to blend in with the locals," I said, gripping the handle.

He turned into the parking lot, throwing sand and gravel as he skidded to a stop. We piled out and took off running toward the pier. "There's the van," Jack shouted. "Where's Amanda and Colette?"

A white panel van slowed to a stop, ready to make the turn onto the pier. I scanned the roadways. No sign of the VW. *Crap, where are they?*

The traffic cleared and the van made the turn. This was our

chance. I looked both ways, up and down the causeway. No VW.

"How do you know that's the right van?" Doug said. "Noah was supposed to make sure we knew which one it was, right?"

"If Claudia got the message to him. And he was able to. And if he did, how?"

"Look." He pointed with the tire iron he carried in his hand.

Another white panel van was coming down the causeway, headed our way. It was the van. No question. Noah was on the roof. I shook my head. I should have known.

I looked the other way. The VW was puttering toward the corner. *C'mon guys, we've got one chance at this.*

The van turned the corner onto the pier, Carlos at the wheel, and Amanda was there with the VW. She gunned it to get right in front of him, then slammed on the brakes. Crash! *Go team! We got him!*

The driver-side door popped open and Carlos was hollering before his feet hit the ground. Amanda and Colette eased out of the VW, clad in bikinis for extra attention, and staggered toward him, hollering back.

You can always count on the crowd to do what crowds do. Clumps of people started to form around the scene. I hid among the throngs. I couldn't be seen.

Doug and Jack closed in. They had to get that back door open before Carlos noticed. Amanda and Colette were doing their part, keeping him distracted. Before Jack and Doug reached the van though, Noah sprang down from the roof, flipped the handle, and swung the panel doors wide. Jack and Doug bounded inside, grabbed a wooden crate, and dragged it onto the road. These guys were good. Noah was prying at the lid with the tire iron. Within seconds, Jack had a second crate, and Doug a third, hauled out onto the road. From where I stood, it looked like that was it. Three crates total.

Carlos came around the side of the van. "¿Qué demonios crees que estás haciendo?" *What the hell do you think you're doing?*

Noah flipped over the first crate and a writhing pile of snakes slid onto the pavement. The crowd reacted with squeals and gasps. Carlos jerked his head toward the witnesses, panic on his face. He had an audience. He had to be careful.

Dan and Sierra materialized from the crowd, one on each side of the van, spray cans in hand, and went to work painting "LIVE FREE!" down the side panels.

"¡Esa es mi propiedad!" Carlos shouted. *That's my property!*

I glanced around the crowd. People stared, motionless. "¡Llame a la policía!" I said to a man standing next to me. *Call the police!* I moved through the crowd. "¡Llame a la policía!" I kept moving. *Get on your phones, people!*

Jack and Doug faced down Carlos while Noah pried the lid off the second crate. Carlos glared at them, then his expression changed as recognition set in. He looked to Jack, then back to Doug, wracked with confusion. I could imagine what was running through his mind. He didn't know what the hell was going on. But he was smart enough to know it was more than a group of harmless activists. His eyes grew large and flitted around.

Noah flipped over the second crate and another clump of slithering snakes wriggled to get free of each other. He immediately went to work on the third crate.

"Keep your hands off that crate," Carlos said in English. "Back off."

Be careful! Noah cracked the lid, flipped it open, and jumped back. That was the one.

Sirens wailed a block away. Noah glared at Carlos and I could tell something wasn't right. *Noah, wait for the police!*

Noah took a step back from the crate. "Screw you!" he said to Carlos. He slammed his foot into the top edge of the crate. It rocked, tipping on its edge. Carlos rushed forward to push it back. He grabbed hold of the open edge with two hands and a snake reared up and struck him on the wrist. He screamed out in pain and dropped to the ground, wailing. The crowd gasped. Carlos rolled around on the pavement, holding his wrist in his hand, blathering in Spanish.

Noah kicked the crate again and knocked it over. The fer-de-lance tumbled from the top and landed in an s-coil next to Carlos. Shrieks and cries of fear rippled through the crowd. The snake uncoiled and shot across the road, the crowd parting for it. It disappeared in the grass.

Left on the road next to Carlos was a tangle of boa constrictors, fat and sluggish. But no drugs.

Noah, Jack and Doug smashed the crate to bits looking for a hidden compartment. Something. But there was nothing else. They ripped apart the other two crates. Nothing.

The police cars came around the corner. Jack and Doug took off at a dead run. Dan and Sierra had already disappeared among the tourists. Noah picked up a boa, then another, scanning the pavement beneath them, shaking his head. There was nothing there.

Dammit! We'd been so sure. The poisonous snake was there. Carlos had been driving, not Paco. What had we missed? I held my head, a sinking sensation threatening to take me down. All this for nothing. *Dammit! Dammit! Dammit!*

I watched helplessly as an officer put Noah in handcuffs and another questioned Amanda and Colette.

This didn't make sense. Why was there a fer-de-lance in the crate if there were no drugs? One poisonous snake. One lousy snake wouldn't bring much on the black market. It was hardly worth the trip. We needed for him to get arrested. But now, especially since he'd been ambushed by activists, he probably wouldn't even get a slap on the wrist for possession.

I smirked. At least the snake had given him more than a slap. But it wouldn't help me catch Maria.

I stared at the boas lying on the ground. Why would he put a poisonous snake in with them? Legal species. The fat, lethargic things barely moved, as if they'd just been fed—*holy crap, that's it!* No wonder Carlos was so confident.

I looked around. Would they confiscate the snakes as evidence? Examine them? What if they didn't?

I stepped from the crowd. "Excuse me, sir," I said to the officer who had cuffed Noah. "I'm sorry to interrupt."

"Quédese atrás," he said, holding his hand out in the universal sign to stop.

"No, no, the snake, look at the snake," I said, pointing.

"I need you to stay back," he said in English, stepping toward me.

I held up my hands. "I understand," I said. "I'm a veterinarian. From the U.S. I just happened to notice, there's something very wrong with these snakes. Do you mind?" I stepped toward the boas.

"Get back," the officer told me, his voice stern.

"But they might die," I pleaded, giving him my best doe eyes. "Please. I just want to check on them. Please."

He looked to the other officer who shrugged.

"Gracias," I said. I got down on my knees and took the fattest boa in my arms. I ran my hands down the length of it until I felt the lump. The snake came to life at my touch and wrapped itself around my waist. Behind the lump, I squeezed, pushing the bulge forward, hand over hand like a tube of toothpaste, working the bulge toward the throat. The snake bucked in my arms. "C'mon, give it up," I told him. I kneaded and rubbed and shoved. I had to get my elbow into it, but managed to get the lump moving toward its mouth.

When it was close, I hollered for the officer to come over. "This snake was fed recently," I said and squeezed as hard as I could below its throat. The snake writhed and jerked, its mouth unhinged and spread open wide, and a red rubber balloon stuffed with drugs plopped out onto the ground.

The cop's eyes grew wide. He told me to drop the snake and back away. I did as I was told. He grabbed the radio from his belt and called it in. I backed away further, then a little further, and into the crowd.

Noah watched me go, a big smile on his face.

Once I was several blocks away, I took out my phone and punched the number for Mom. Mr. Strix answered in one ring. "Carlos Mendoza was just arrested for running drugs—"

"How in the world do you know that?"

"It happened right on the street. Everyone saw it." I had a short window. Carlos was in excruciating pain, so they'd take him straight to the hospital for the antidote, but eventually on to the police station. "Is there any chance you could keep him from making any calls? Have the customs authority hold him for questioning or something. Forty-eight hours would be great."

"I can try, but why—"

"I have a hunch."

CHAPTER 16

The cooler had been dragged out to the bonfire. Everyone was there, drinking in celebration. Everyone except Noah.

"Even though they saw the drugs, they still arrested Noah," I said.

Doug, tipping a beer, waved it off. He wiped his mouth with the back of his hand and said, "Noah'll be fine. He's been arrested before. No big deal."

Jack handed me a beer. "He'll be out in twenty-four hours."

I hoped they were right. I couldn't do anything for him without jeopardizing my job. I looked to Amanda and Colette. "Did you get the phone?"

"Right here," Colette said and dug it out of her handbag. "It was in the cab of the truck."

"Good," I said. I scrolled through the numbers to find Maria's. "Excellent. Amanda, you have the web thing ready?"

"Yep," she said and handed me a slip of paper. "Here's the URL."

I handed it and the phone to Doug. "You're up."

Doug took the phone and grinned. He drew in a long breath and his expression changed to one of a ruthless drug dealer. "Okay, I'm ready," he said.

He punched send and held the phone to his ear. We all waited, silent. After a few moments, he said, "Listen to me very carefully. Your brother has been a very naughty boy. If you ever want to see him alive again, you'll pay what he owes. Two hundred thousand dollars." He listened. "Well, you see, the thing is, my boss is not a patient man. By midnight. Or he dies." He looked at me as he listened, his eyebrows raised. Then finally, "Good. You'll transfer the money through a web site. I'm only going to give you this address once. Are you ready?" There was a long pause then he rattled off the URL. "And just in case he means less to you than we thought, we'll come for those sweet little dogs next." He disconnected.

I let out my breath.

"What'd you think?" he grinned. "What'd you think about the dogs? Nice touch, huh?"

I took the phone from him and ripped it open. I took out the battery and smashed the chip with a rock, then threw it into the fire. "Now we wait," I said. "You guys were fantastic today. I can't thank you enough."

Colette laughed. "I'm not sure the VW fared well, but it was worth it. Noah won't care."

"What if she doesn't pay?" Amanda asked.

"She will," I said.

"But I don't understand," she said. "Why'd you have her pay a ransom?"

"Pressure. I want to tick her off. A hit in the pocketbook ought to do the trick. Not to mention she wants to strangle Carlos herself right about now." I grinned. "But most of all, she's worried, wondering how much this new guy on the block will impact her business. I wouldn't want to be at her house right now."

"Yeah, she's probably pacing in circles, making her little dogs dizzy," Doug said with a grin.

"Now what?" asked Jack. "We storm her house?"

"Now we wait." I shook my head. I couldn't believe these guys.

Jack nodded and apparently felt waiting was a good time to be drinking because he flipped the top off the cooler and started passing cold bottles around.

My phone buzzed. It was Dalton. "Excuse me," I said and walked toward the tree house. "Hello?"

"Hey, it's me," he said. "What are you up to?"

"I'm, uh, at the beach. Enjoying a virgin margarita."

"Yeah, George cancelled cards tonight."

Interesting. "Did he say why?"

"No, but he seemed irritated about something."

Good. Very good.

"I thought maybe we could get dinner."

Are you serious? Just what I need right now. "Okay," I said. What else could I say? "I'll meet you back at the bungalow."

I shuffled back down to the fire. "I've gotta go," I said.

"What? What about Maria and the ransom?"

"You'll have to let me know."

Dalton was showered, shaved, and all dressed up. "Let's go someplace nice," he said.

I changed into the cotton sundress, the only remotely formal attire I had, and we headed for the restaurant at the Playa de Delfines resort. Dalton pulled up to the front door, got out of the car and ran around to open my door for me. He offered his arm and we entered the restaurant, happy newlyweds, as the valet drove away with the car.

Candles flickered atop tables covered with white linens. The aroma of fresh fish and seafood wafted on the sea breeze. The clink of silverware on fine china mixed with the murmur of intimate conversations.

We got to our table, a table for two on the deck overlooking the ocean, and Dalton pulled out my chair for me. He certainly was making an effort.

As he sat, he said to the waiter, "We'd like a bottle of wine. The lady will choose."

I smiled. "Your house red will be fine. Thank you."

I looked at Dalton and he looked at me. He seemed nervous. A Navy SEAL, nervous. "I was hoping…" He made sure he had my attention. "I was hoping we could start over."

He continued to surprise me. "How do you mean?"

"I tried to apologize today and, well, I blew it." He managed an uncomfortable grin. "Obviously."

I shook my head. "You didn't blow it. It was me." *Oh man!* "My mom always said I could hold a grudge."

"I didn't exactly give you a reason to like me," he said, his voice thick.

I smiled. "That's for sure."

He let out a short, half laugh, a sigh of relief really. "Yeah."

I grinned. The candlelight was warm, cozy. "You're kinda growing on me, though."

The waiter arrived with the wine. He poured the test sample. I sipped. It was fine. I gave him a nod, then he poured a glass for each of us. Dalton raised his, taking hold of it by the stem this time I noticed. "To a fresh start," he said.

I lifted my glass to meet his. "To a fresh start."

His eyes met mine and they softened. "I was an ass. I'm sorry."

"Yes, you were." I grinned. "But I've been a pain in the ass, too, so, you know."

He laughed, a light, easy laugh. I could tell he was already feeling relaxed. He smiled and his eyes seemed to light up. "I know what you're feeling. It's frustrating. But you'll make it to Special Ops someday. No doubt in my mind. You've got what it takes. I can see it in you. It just takes patience."

"Yeah, patience," I said. "Not exactly my strong suit."

"It'll happen." He smiled again and I noticed how the color of his eyes seemed to change from brown to a hazel-green, taking on the hue of the green shirt that fit snuggly over his shoulders. I pictured him in his dress uniform, crisp and cut. My cheeks flushed. I felt like one of those cheerleaders, swooning over the hot soldier who was home on leave.

"What?" he said. "I mean it. You'll be great."

"Thanks," I said. I glanced at my phone. No word yet from Amanda. "What made you want to be an agent? For that matter, what made you want to be a SEAL?"

"Oh, you know. Why does any SEAL want to be a SEAL?"

I nodded. They were a different breed, that was for sure.

"I knew I couldn't be a career SEAL, though. I mean, I loved the job, don't get me wrong. But I wanted to have another life, you know, kids." He shrugged, disappointment in his face.

"But your marriage…?"

"Navy wives," he said, matter-of-fact.

I grew up a Navy brat. I knew exactly what he meant. "I'm sorry," I said. "The crack about your divorce the other day crossed the line. I'm really sorry."

He nodded. "It is what it is." He shook his head. "And the girls back home…"

"Where's home?"

"Montana. I grew up hunting and fishing. Loved the outdoors."

I nodded. A lot of Fish and Wildlife agents had similar backgrounds.

He took another sip of wine. "As far as the undercover work, well, I've got no ties and I'm good at it."

I glanced at my phone. Nothing.

"Do you have somewhere to be?" he asked.

"What? Why?"

"The phone."

"Oh, no. Just checking the time."

His brows raised. He wasn't satisfied with my answer.

"Sorry, habit I guess." I tucked it under my thigh so I'd feel it vibrate if I got a text. "I just realized," I said. "I don't even know your first name."

His expression didn't change. "Everyone calls me Dalton."

"Isn't that your last name?"

He nodded slightly. "You can call me Dalton."

"All right." *Mental note. Dig into that story.*

I smiled. He smiled. There was a big awkward space you could steer a cruise ship through.

The waiter arrived to take our order. I chose the Pasta Primavera and Dalton ordered the Surf and Turf—tenderloin, rare, and grilled lobster.

I sneaked a peek at my phone. Nothing. I glanced at Dalton and suddenly felt like a complete fool. What if what I'd done backfired? What if I blew our cover to smithereens and everything he'd been working toward? Or worse?

I shook it off. *She'll pay. She's gonna pay. And then she'll come running to us.*

"So what's your story?"

He caught me off guard. "What?"

"You're a vegetarian." He gave me a sympathetic smile. "By the way, that first night, I felt bad for you, but you were a trooper, chewing away on that prime rib."

I smirked.

"Don't worry. No one else noticed."

"Yeah, but how'd you know?"

He cocked his head to the side. "I was sitting right next to you."

I sighed. Damn. I thought I'd covered pretty well.

"I know you're into yoga. But that's it. Oh, and you were a Navy brat. Overseas?"

"My mom was a physician on the Mercy. We were in the Philippines for awhile." I hesitated. He didn't need my whole life story. "High school in San Diego. Which SEAL team were you?"

"Three."

"So you were West Coast."

He nodded, impressed. "That's right. But you're changing the subject back to me. You're good at that."

I shrugged. It was true. I twirled my bracelet around my wrist.

"That's a beautiful bracelet," he said. "I've noticed you never take it off."

I nodded. "My father gave it to me. It was the last..." I looked into Dalton's eyes. "It was the last time I saw him." I shook my head. "I should have been there with him."

"What do you mean? What happened?"

I shook my head. "I was in school, my freshman year. I should have been there with him. If he hadn't been alone..."

Dalton waited, giving me time before finally asking, "What are you saying?"

"My father was killed by poachers. I know it. I was told it was an accident, but I know where he was. They'd threatened him in the past, but my dad, he was stubborn."

"Poppy, listen to me. If you'd have been there, you probably would have been killed, too."

I stared off into space, into the past, when my phone buzzed and I jerked in my seat. Dalton eyed me with suspicion.

"You know," he said. "Maria came out to the golf course this evening. She seemed agitated."

"Oh?" I said and took a gulp of wine.

"She talked to George, then he canceled the card game with no explanation, and she led him away by the nose."

"Really? What do you think that was all about?"

"I don't know, but we leave day after tomorrow. Maybe tomorrow morning you should stop in, make friends. See what you can find out. You can ride over with me."

"All right," I said. No way. I couldn't go there tomorrow morning. If I showed up on her doorstep, it would ruin everything I had going. She had to call me. I'd have to think of an excuse. "I should take something. I saw a bakery in town. We could stop on the way and get a torta chilena or something."

He eyed me and I couldn't read what he was thinking. "Okay," he finally said.

Our dinner arrived. As the waiter placed Dalton's plate in front of him, I stole a second to glance down at my phone. Text from Amanda read: Done.

I raised my wine glass and held it in front of me. "Here's to working with you," I said. "It's been, well, an experience."

He laughed. "Yeah, I'll say."

As we ate our meals, I decided I really liked Dalton. I was feeling more comfortable with him. Too bad I'd probably never see him again after we left Costa Rica in two days.

Neither of us wanted dessert, so he called for the car and we headed back to our room. He parked and got out to open my door again. "Let's take a walk," he said and took me by the hand. He led me down by the pool to a deck that looked out over the valley. Tiny solar lights lit the walkway and gave a warm glow to the night. The insects croaked away in the thicket, the warm air full of the scents of the floral garden. He leaned on the railing and turned to face me. "Nice view, huh?"

"Yes," I said. I could barely see him in the faint moonlight but the glow of Arenal Volcano stood out in the dark sky.

"Don't look now but," he whispered, "we're being watched."

"Oh?" I hadn't seen Yipes or anyone around when we got out of the car. How had I missed him?

"Kiss me," he said and pulled me to him. His lips met mine, a gentle caress, then he pulled me tighter, passion rising. It's too dark for anyone to see, I realized, mid-kiss. But I didn't care. I wanted his kiss. I wanted his arms around me. He pulled away for a moment, as if he were giving me the chance to back away, as though he knew that I knew no one was really watching. I hesitated. "I'm sorry," he whispered. "I—"

I wrapped my hands around his neck and pressed my lips to his and I was like a teenager, back in high school at the homecoming dance. My nerves tingled. Oh he could kiss! I leaned into him, pressing my body against his. He held me tight, his hands at the small of my back. I remembered how he'd lifted me up and twirled me around in the airport. Strong but gentle. His kiss was like that, strong but gentle. A flush of warmth came over me and I wanted to give into it. I wanted him to take me back to our room. I wanted to feel his hands on me, to—I pulled away to catch my breath.

"We probably shouldn't—" I bit down hard on my lip.

"I know," he said and nuzzled my neck.

"I mean, essentially, you're my boss and—"

"Yeah," he said, his head nodding in agreement. "You're right." But he didn't let me go from his embrace.

"We should call it a night," I said. "Head back to the room." I pinched my lips together. "I mean…you know what I mean."

I couldn't see his expression in the dark, couldn't tell what he was thinking, but his breathing changed and he held me against him as though he didn't want to let go. Finally, he nodded and we walked straight back to the room. He shut the door behind him and I was in his arms again. This time he pulled away. "I thought you said—"

"Shut up and kiss me," I said. He grinned. "No wait," I said. *Crap!*

I spun around and took a few steps away, then turned back to face him. His eyes had turned to a soft brown. He looked at me, waiting, his breath coming in short pants.

"I'm not sure we should—I mean, you and I—we probably ought to…"

He nodded.

"I'm going to take a shower," I said. I escaped to the bathroom and locked the door behind me. I looked in the mirror. My hair was all frizzed out. *This humidity has messed with more than your hair. Your damn hormones are on the fritz.* I cranked on the cold water.

Chapter 17

I left the bungalow early under the guise of wanting to get to the bakery before they were sold out. I told Dalton to wait, I'd be back. I didn't want him to catch me pacing and I didn't want him going to the house. Maria hadn't called yet and I was starting to wonder if she would. Either way, I was leaving tomorrow, back to the U.S., back to the grind, back to working my way up from the bottom. As Dalton had made clear, this was a one-time deal, a necessity wrung from a senior agent's mistake.

My plan had to work.

I climbed the stairs to the tree house. Noah hadn't been back yet and the place had a lonely aura. So small, so primitive. I went to the bathroom and gave the biscuit can a shake. I grinned with absolute, unadulterated relief when Clyde bounded up the side of the house and swung on the hammock, launching himself into position to catch a biscuit.

"There you are," I said. I lobbed a biscuit into the air and he caught it. I watched him gnaw at it, holding it in his little hand and stump. I marveled at his ability to cope without his right hand. He compensated well. After all, what choice did he have? "Life is suffering," I said. "That's what the Buddha said." He didn't look my way, didn't look up from his biscuit. He lived in the moment. That peace for which we strive, he'd mastered. Live for today. Live and let live. "If only others could share your wisdom," I said.

I went out onto the balcony, leaned on the railing, and gazed out at the ocean. "Oh, Clyde, what if she doesn't call?" The morning sun streamed down into the water making it glow an aquamarine. "I'll never have this chance again." I turned back to Clyde. He was swallowing the last crumb. "Maybe I should have listened to Dalton. Maybe I should tell him what I've done. I think he'll understand."

Clyde jumped onto the railing beside me and bobbed up and down, chittering away, his way of communicating.

"I'm just trying to make a difference, you know." Clyde grinned at me, his round, black eyes looking into mine, like he knew. "You're lucky now, little buddy. You have Isabella. And Noah." I frowned. Noah. What was I going to do about him?

"I don't think I'll ever see you again, Clyde. This is goodbye, you know. Adiós." Clyde frowned, covered his eyes with his tiny hand, and shook his head. "Isabella must have taught you the word adiós, huh?" He shook his head again. "Oh Clyde." I picked him up, sat down in the chair, and cuddled him in my lap. "I'll miss you." I stroked his head and he cooed. I laid my head back, enjoying the warm morning scents, and warmth of another being, loving me. It was simple. "You're the perfect man, Clyde," I said. "Those other guys, complicated. But not you." I scratched behind his ear. "Not you."

The phone rang. I jerked in the seat. Clyde leaped from my lap. I looked at my cell. Unknown number. "Hello?"

"Brittany, this is George."

"Hi, George." Of course she'd have George call.

"Maria mentioned that you might be interested in looking at some animals yourself?"

"Oh that," I gave him a Brittany giggle. "No need. I'm all set. Thanks anyway." I hung up.

I gave Clyde a scratch on the head. "Time to talk to Dalton," I said and headed for my moped.

He was in the bathroom when I got there. I paced around the room, doubting, rethinking how I was going to tell him. The door opened. "We need to talk," I said.

"I know last night was—"

"What? No. This isn't about last night."

He looked confused. "All right, what then?"

"George just called me. He offered to show me some more animals."

"What? George? Called *you*? Why would he call you? What did he say?" He paused. "Are you sure it was him?"

"He said Maria told him to call me."

Dalton's brow knit with confusion.

I shifted on my feet. "Maria believes I'm the one making decisions on the big ticket buys."

He stared at me for a long, thoughtful moment, then his expression turned to annoyance. His temper in check, he forced out the words, "And why would she think that?"

I offered a don't-be-too-upset grin. "I kinda told her that."

His jaw tightened and he asked through clenched teeth, "And why would you do that?"

"She cornered me in the horse barn. She knew I spoke Spanish. She accused me of hiding something." I gave up on the grin. "So I went on the offensive."

He spun around, ran his fingers through his hair, and gripped a handful at the top of his scalp. "Please, tell me what you mean by offensive."

"Nothing really, I just tried to connect with her, you know, psychology 101. Since she's really in charge, and George is her lackey, I figured if I made her think I had really been faking the ditzy wife thing, give her a good reason, you know, the redirect, she'd understand and we'd bond."

"Bond?" He spun back around to face me. "You're not making any sense. And why didn't you tell me this before?"

I held his gaze. I had no answer. At least one I could tell him.

"Tell me everything."

"That's about it really."

"Why don't I believe you?" He paced toward the window and back. "So where did George say to meet and when?"

"He didn't."

"What do you mean? I thought you said he called with an offer."

"He did. I turned him down."

"You what?" He grabbed his hair again and laced his fingers together. He looked like he was holding the top of his head so it wouldn't blow off. "Why would you—"

"You don't bite at the first offer."

"Gee, don't tell me, Negotiation 101?"

"Actually, I saw it on an episode of MacGyver," I said, deadpan. He didn't need to be a total jerk.

He held out his hands like he wanted to grab me by the neck.

"Don't worry. She's going to call me herself."

His cheeks were turning red. "And how the hell do you know that?"

"Trust me. She will."

He plopped down in the chair, his mouth hanging open.

"I worked hard to make her think I'm a hard-nosed business woman. If I told George yes, she would suspect something was up. No good businessman would jump at the first offer." He stared at me, unblinking. "Only a cop would do that."

His expression turned to disdain.

My cell phone rang. "See," I said. "Right on time." I picked up. "Howdie," I said in a cheerful Brittany voice.

Dalton flopped back in the chair with a groan.

It was Maria. In a calm, clear voice she said, "I'm confident we can come to an arrangement that will suit your needs."

"I've already made arrangements that suit my needs," I said. Dalton covered his face with his hands.

"I tell you what," she said. "Hear me out. We already have an established relationship. Take a look at my merchandise. I will match any other offer or beat it. What have you got to lose?"

"Hold on," I said. I held my hand over the phone and winked at Dalton. He shook his head. I sang a verse of *Row, Row, Row your Boat* in my head. That was probably a good amount of time. I put the phone back to my ear. "All right," I said. "We might as well take a look."

CHAPTER 18

I mentioned to Dalton on the way to Maria's house that we should stop and pick up a torta chilena. I don't know why, but that seemed to irritate him more.

He felt the need to remind me of our goal. "We are to confirm she is the head of this operation. Nothing else. We don't reveal ourselves. We keep our cover. Nash decides what to do with the information. Do you understand?"

"Perfectly."

"I mean it, Poppy. We're not in the U.S. Our goal here is not an arrest. Our goal is intel. That's it."

"I understand." I got it the first time.

"Even if we get an offer to sell, we do not arrest, we do not hint at arrest. We don't warn, talk, sing. We do nothing."

"Got it. No singing."

He yanked the steering wheel to the right and skidded to a halt on the side of the road. He spun in the seat to face me. I instinctively pulled back from him. He was pretty fired up and I had no idea what was coming.

"Let me be very clear," he said, his jaw set. "I don't like this. I don't like how this has transpired. How you've—" He sneered. "I'm damn sure there's more you're not telling me. But we are going in there together. And there is no question about it, our lives are in danger. Do you understand that? Do you?"

I nodded. I did.

He stared ahead, his hands gripping the wheel for some time, then shook his head, reluctantly coming to some conclusion. "You got the invitation, however you did it. If she believes you're the one running the show, then—" he clenched his jaw, then let out a breath "—then we need to continue with that. You need to take the lead." He looked down, his tongue stuck in his cheek. "I'll act the clueless husband."

I couldn't believe what I was hearing. I had underestimated him. He was a true professional, dedicated to the mission—no matter what it took.

"Just remember," he said, his finger in my face. "My life is in your hands."

I nodded.

"I need to know you understand. I need to hear you say it."

I looked into his eyes. "I know this is not a game. I know it's dangerous. I promise to be careful."

He seemed somewhat relieved. "You better be."

I held his gaze, serious. I nodded.

He eyed me. "What else do I need to know?"

That I made her believe there's another kingpin in town, threatening to take over her business. That I tricked her into paying a ransom. That I put Carlos in jail for running drugs. "Nothing," I said. "I swear."

"All right." He seemed satisfied.

"I didn't mean to—" I sighed. "I just knew she was the kingpin and the opportunity was there and—"

"What's done is done." He stared ahead for a long time, thinking. It was as though some of the events of the past few days were clicking into place, making sense to him. "Believe me, I've been there. I just wish you would've told me before." He stared, thought some more. Then turned to me, his expression stern, as though to drive home the point. "Remember what I said? This whole business of working under cover is like improv. So now, whatever happens, whatever is said, we go with it. No matter what happens, we stay in character."

"I can do improv."

"Not just improv. The most important skill you can have—more important than any combat training, physical strength, or technical skills—is your ability to twist the truth to fit the situation, to shape it to your advantage. On the fly." He grinned. "And the ability to sell it. Which," he shook his head, "I have no doubt you can do."

He slammed the gearshift into drive and pulled out. "Let's do this thing."

As we pulled into the drive, the butler stepped onto the porch and called the guard dogs off. We parked and got out of the car. The butler greeted us. "She is waiting for you in the horse barn," he said with a smile, as if we were there for afternoon tea.

Dalton took me by the hand and, as we walked toward the barn, he leaned over and kissed me on the cheek. "For luck," he whispered.

As we entered the barn, part of me feared this was a farce, that she wouldn't be there. That all my work had been for nothing. But she was waiting.

If she hadn't been an evil wildlife smuggler, I'd have admired her poise. She carried herself with a confidence most women would envy. She was neither friendly nor stand-offish. She simply welcomed us.

Her little dogs circled, yipping their hellos. The same man was with her, the one who carried the gun. "Ramon will hold your cell phones," she said.

Dalton handed his over without reluctance. I dug around in the bottom of my handbag for mine. Fortunately, I'd erased all the texts and numbers already. "Search her bag, too," Maria said.

I shrugged and handed him the bag. "Keep it," I said. If he

searched it, some items might give him pause. This way, he'd be less likely to bother. I didn't like being without those items, but you do what you've got to do.

Maria gestured to three horses that had been saddled and were ready to ride. "Let's go then." Maria made it look easy. She seemed to float onto the back of the horse. Her man picked up each dog and they were placed in the saddle bags on either side of her, their little heads poking out.

Dalton helped me mount my horse. Not that I needed help. Then he heaved himself atop his.

We followed Maria out of the barn and down a trail, the trail that led to the neighboring property and the coffee-roasting shed. She wasn't hiding now. Maybe it was arrogance. Maybe she figured I knew now anyway. What was there to hide? Either way, she was taking us directly to her hidden lair and, I was sure, going to offer some class I species—scarlet macaws, howler monkeys, ridley turtles, maybe even a jaguar. If we were really lucky, she'd offer shark fins, but that was unlikely, since we'd established we were in the pet market. One step at a time.

I felt a divine sense of satisfaction. She was leading us to our goal, to confirmation. Yet, at the same time, it felt hollow. We'd get up to the shed, see the illegal animals, confirm she was the kingpin, then we'd smile and walk away. I wanted to see her in handcuffs, dragged off to prison for what she does. I couldn't help it; I wanted her to suffer for every animal she'd ever harmed.

At one o' clock in the afternoon, the heat was more than uncomfortable. The horses labored, huffing with sweat. Maria didn't seem to care. She pushed her horse up the inclines and we had to keep up. She said nothing. Simply led and we followed.

Finally, with my blouse soaked with sweat and my inner thighs raw from rubbing the saddle (of course I wore shorts), we came into the clearing where the roasting shed stood amid the concrete slabs. We dismounted and a guard led the horses to a shaded area with a trough.

I tried to hide my excitement. This was it. Once Dalton saw the class I species inside, there'd be no question she was the kingpin.

Maria led us around the corner of the shed and as we stepped inside I stopped short and my knees turned to jelly. It was empty. The two old coffee roasters stood in the corner and that was it.

She gestured toward a couple of folding chairs. "Have a seat."

What was this about? I glanced at Dalton. He acted the dopey husband, as he'd said he would. He happily grabbed a chair and popped it open, placing it in front of me, then set up another for himself. He plopped down as if he didn't have a care in the world.

"Before we go any further," she said. "I just want to clarify a few things." Her eyes bore into me. I met her gaze, as steely eyed as she was. "You came for a monkey, did you not?"

Dalton grinned. "Yeah, my sweetheart wants her own." He beamed at me, love in his eyes. At least *he* was following our plan. What was Maria up to?

Maria smiled demurely at Dalton. "John, dear, I hate to be the one to tell you, but your wife has been a very busy lady making some arrangements of her own." She stepped closer to him and ran her fingers through his hair. "And here, I thought we had something special."

"What?" My head snapped toward Dalton. "What's she talking about?"

He pursed his lips. "Nothing, honey bunny." He grinned wide. "Sweetheart." He glared at Maria. "She's trying to drive a wedge between us of mistrust." He shook it off. "It's an old business tactic. Don't fall for it." He looked her in the eyes. "Our deal stands. You know I'm willing to pay a fair price. Let's just see what you've got."

I eyed him, then looked back to her. She wore a sly grin.

Maybe I should give her what she wants. See where this leads.

"What's going on, John?"

"Nothing." He wouldn't look at me. "I said don't worry about it."

I drew in a sharp breath and covered my mouth. "You've been sleeping with her!" *Holy crap, I didn't see that one coming.*

"Oh, honey, can't you see? She's making you—"

"Don't you *honey* me." I turned my back to him.

"Oh, you're one to talk," he said.

I spun around and glared at him. *What the hell is he doing?* He crossed his arms and huffed, like he was trying to get up the nerve to say something. "You'll sleep with any young stud with a ponytail."

My mouth dropped open. "How dare you?"

"You think I don't know? You sneaking off during the day to get some action. While I'm working to put food on the table. You promised you'd stop. This trip was supposed to be for us." He managed a hopeful grin. "To bring us together."

I clamped my mouth shut. I didn't know what to say. I had to trust Dalton. He had just reminded me, improv was the cornerstone of undercover work. Go with it. But what the hell was going on? I looked to Maria. She stood with her arms crossed, a smug expression on her face, nodding approvingly. She was enjoying this.

I glared at Dalton and said through gritted teeth. "You have the nerve to accuse me. And you've been with"—I jerked my head toward Maria—"*her*."

He shrugged, a noncommittal, it-doesn't-matter-anymore shrug. "Can we just do some business here? Talk about this later?"

My mind went into overdrive. What does Maria think she knows? After I'd confronted her, had she tried to seduce Dalton to probe him for information about me? Or had he been sleeping with her all along? And if so, what had he been planning? Wait—he said ponytail. *Noah.* But why would he give him away? *Unless Maria already knows. That means—*

"Yes, let's get to business," said Maria. "I have just the right pet for you." She brought her fingers to her lips and whistled, one of those loud whistles that can be heard in the next county.

One of the guards came through the door carrying a cage with a cloth draped over the top. He set it down next to her and stood behind her, his hand on the weapon strapped over his shoulder. The cage was situated so the door faced away from me. I couldn't see what was inside. Maria opened the cage, reached in, grabbed hold, and rose to face us with a monkey in her grasp, her hand wrapped around its tiny neck. A white-faced capuchin. Squirming and squealing. It's little hands reached up to grip her wrist and I saw it. The right hand was missing.

Oh my god. It's Clyde.

Maria grinned with evil pleasure. She shook Clyde, tightening her grip around his neck, and he let out a shriek. "What do you think?"

My gut turned to water. *Think. Think! What the hell is going on?* Poor little Clyde. *She knows all about Noah and Isabella too! Dammit!* Of course she'd know who was targeting her operation. But Dalton must have known something, somehow. He covered with the adultery story. But how? Why hadn't he mentioned it to me?

She must think I'm an activist, an eco-terrorist. It was the only thing that made sense.

Clyde whimpered. Maria gave him another shake. "¡Cállate!" *Shut up!*

My breath came in short pants. *Not Clyde!* I wanted to grab Maria by the neck and shake her, shake her until her brains spilled out. But I couldn't. I couldn't move, couldn't act. Instead, I had to convince her I was a slutty, rich bitch who'd sleep with anything for sport. That Noah was a coincidence. If she thought I was an activist, here to infiltrate her operation, she'd kill us both. Dalton knew it, too.

I glared at him. "Are we still on the monkey kick?" I added

an eye roll. "I never wanted a frigging monkey. That was your idea. But you couldn't let it go." I crossed my arms. "*Oh, darling, let's have a baby,*" I mocked. "Don't you get it. I only married you because I got pregnant. And you were so—" I shook my head. "So damn sweet. Then we lost the baby anyway." I rolled my eyes again. "But Jesus, can you be any more boring in the bedroom? The lights always have to be out, really? Always on top? My god, screwing a Hobbit would be more exciting than you." I blew out my breath. *Where do I come up with this stuff?*

His bottom lip quivered. "You always have to do that, don't you. Emasculate me in front of other women."

"Emasculate? Wow, been working on your vocabulary, have you?"

"Oh, you think I'm stupid? I knew you were sleeping with him the moment I saw him. The way he looked at you. You don't care about me. You don't care about him. You only care about the size of his—"

"Enough!" We both jerked our heads toward Maria. She held Clyde up and shook him again. He squirmed in her grasp, his little eyes begging me to help. I couldn't. *I can't.* If I showed any emotion, any sign of caring about him, we'd all be dead. I turned back to Dalton so I wouldn't have to look at Clyde's pleading eyes. "Jerk," I said, acting as though I was too mad at him to even notice the monkey.

"Bitch," he muttered back.

"What'd you call me?" *Keep it up. Keep the attention from Clyde. Maybe we'll all get out of this alive.*

Dalton grew silent, solemn. He put his head down. "All I've ever wanted was for you to be happy, for you to have special things."

"Well, *honey bunny*, all you need to do then is shut up." I turned my attention back to Maria. "You dragged us up here in this god-awful heat." I pulled my wet blouse from my skin. "Look at me. I need a shower." I shot her a look of disgust. "Do you have an offer or what?"

She didn't miss a beat. "Right now, I'm offering you this monkey." Her eyes bore into me like a dentist's probe, poking into the dark crevices of my thoughts, scraping at my emotions. "What do you think? Do you have a buyer for him?"

"Don't waste my time," I said. "I told you. I'm only interested in big ticket pets. Exotics. I can get a monkey anywhere."

Her eyes narrowed. "You're right," she said. I breathed a little. "These are a dime a dozen. Besides"—she held up his right hand—"this one is damaged. Worthless." She rubbed the top of his head with one hand and tightened her grip on his neck. His tiny tongue stuck out from his mouth. Her eyes locked on me and she said, "Another mouth to feed." With a quick jerk of her wrist, she snapped his neck and tossed him to the floor at my feet. His little body landed with a thwack.

The breath left my body. I stared, way too long. Clyde lay still, a tiny pool of blood forming under his head. I tried to find my voice. All I could think about were soldiers, soldiers who give their lives for liberty, for freedom, for justice for all. Young boys who go off to war, for a promise of amber waves of grain, of purple mountain majesties, for a land of the free and the home of the brave, willing to give the ultimate sacrifice. For a cause. For something they believed in. For their brothers.

Poor Clyde. I could not let his death be in vain. I would not. *For your brothers, Clyde.*

I raised my chin and looked her in the eye. "What the hell woman? You almost got that on my shoe."

Dalton shook his head and muttered, "Heartless bitch."

I turned my gaze on him so I could think without her seeing my eyes. This was a test. Just a test. I drew in a deep breath. *Hold it together, McVie. Think!*

Okay. None of this changed the fact that she was desperate to sell. She'd brought us this far. She must've had a plan once we passed the test. If she had class I species, they couldn't be crated, ignored for days, then transported like snakes and frogs.

They'd need regular care. They had to be housed somewhere. I was betting it was nearby. And we're here now.

I huffed an annoyed huff. "You're wasting my time."

Maria studied me as though she still wasn't convinced. I rose from the chair. "C'mon, John. Let's go."

He got up and followed me toward the door.

Maria followed right behind us. "Now let's not be too hasty," she said.

I shrugged as though I really didn't care either way.

She passed between us and turned and motioned for us to return to the shed. "I'm sure you understand, in this business, I can't be too careful." I knew it. This was really happening. "I'll have my man bring some samples right away." She whistled again.

A guard came around the far corner of the shed and headed toward us with a two-way radio in his hand. He nodded to Maria, then looked right at me. It was the guy, the one who had chased Noah, the one I clobbered. *Crap!* I dropped my head, but it was too late. He recognized me. "Es ella. ¡Esa es la chica!" he shouted and raised his weapon.

Dalton looked at me. "What's—"

"Run!"

CHAPTER 19

Bullets zinged past me—pop, pop, pop—as I sprinted double-time across the concrete slabs. I plunged into the wall of green, branches and leaves whipping at my face.

Dalton was right behind me. I could barely hear Maria shouting commands to her guards, telling one to follow the ridge, another to follow the tree line and flank us.

I tore through a tangle of vines, dodged tree trunks, and ducked under broad-leafed palms, my lungs burning, my heartbeat banging in my ears.

At once, I realized Dalton wasn't with me anymore. I whipped around. He was limping toward me, his pant leg soaked with blood at his ankle. "You're hit," I said. As he neared, I noticed blood dripping at his elbow, too.

He didn't slow. "I'm fine."

"You're not fine. We can't run like this."

"You can. Go."

No women in combat burst into my head. Then our whole conversation. I looked into his eyes and realized he'd purposely run directly behind me, shielding me from the gunfire. *Oh, Dalton!*

Pop, pop, pop came the crackle of gunfire. I couldn't think about that now. I turned my head one way, then the other, listening. She'd sent them to flank us. That meant they'd separated, spread out. That was good. I looked around to get my bearings. To the right, about twenty paces should be a bell alarm. To the left, one at about fifty paces. "Can you make it about—"

"I'm fine."

"Okay." I nodded. "Okay, follow me," I whispered. "I have an idea."

We moved through the foliage like predators. My dad had taught me how to stalk prey, how to hide, how to become one with the forest and sneak up on a subject without making a noise. Dalton was a SEAL, so, needless to say, I had to keep checking to be sure he was behind me.

I came upon the bell wire and held out my hand to halt Dalton. I pointed down. He saw it and nodded. I stepped back to whisper, "We need to draw them in."

He frowned. "There are five of them, armed. We're outnumbered."

"They're not military. They're boys with guns."

He held his right hand at his left shoulder where a blood stain had formed and winced. "Yeah? How do you know?"

I heard movement behind us. "No time. Fall down and act hurt."

He glared at me with big eyes. "I'm not going to put myself in a prone position."

The sound of a weapon, scraping through foliage was near by. We both heard it.

"Trust me," I said. He hesitated. I stepped on the wire, enough that the bell made a light tinkle that only someone close by could hear.

Dalton gritted his teeth.

I gestured for him to go down.

He regarded me with a cold examination. No doubt, he was running through the tactical advantages, remembering my skill at hand-to-hand combat, sizing me up against the probable skill of the guard who was now twenty paces away and closing.

In an instant, he spun around, grabbed some branches and

stumbled, flailing at leaves as he went, then tumbled to the ground with a grunt.

The guard halted. He'd heard him. He launched into a run toward us.

I dropped to all fours. The guard barreled by. I lunged at him from behind, catching him right in the knees. He collapsed, face down in front of me. I crawled on top of him. He tried to roll, but he was encumbered by his weapon. I pinned his hands to the ground. Dalton crawled toward us and wrenched the weapon free. He flipped it around and trained it on the guy. The guard put his head down. "¡No disparen! Me rindo. Me rindo." *Don't shoot! I surrender. I surrender.*

I scanned the forest floor. A thin vine ran up the side of a nearby tree trunk. I grabbed hold of it, ripped a length from the tree, and wrapped it around his wrists. I pulled his legs up to his back and tied his ankles together and to his wrists.

Dalton smirked. "Been cattle ropin' much?"

"Hey, he's not going anywhere."

Dalton checked the magazine. "Five rounds."

I nodded, but I really didn't want to have to shoot anyone.

There was movement to my left. I looked at Dalton. He'd heard it, too. He scooted to get his back against a tree. I rolled under some ferns.

The guard came running, tromping through the jungle like a bull elephant in rut. I stuck out my foot and he tripped, performing some kind of sideways triple salchow maneuver. I got to my feet to pounce, but he swiped my ankle with a well-executed leg sweep. I fell into the ferns, tucked and rolled, and I was back on my feet. He was scampering along on his hands and knees, one arm out, groping around in front of him. He'd dropped his weapon.

I jumped onto his back, slamming him to the ground just as he'd found the gun. Pop, pop, pop. Bullets zipped through the leaves. I wrapped my arm around his neck and got him in a chokehold. He bucked and flipped me over on my back, the full weight of him on top of me.

A third guard appeared, his weapon pointed at us. He was the one who'd recognized me. The guy I was holding with his belly facing the gun grunted a terrified, "¡No disparen!" *Don't shoot!*

Dalton fired. The bullet grazed the guard's shoulder. Purposefully no doubt. These men weren't trying to kill us. The man threw down his weapon and his hands shot upward.

Dalton motioned with his rifle for him to get down on the ground. I rolled my opponent off of me. He put his hands behind his back, anxious for me to tie him up. I quickly wrapped their wrists with some vine like I had done with the first guy.

Dalton scanned the forest. "Something's not right. That was too easy."

I sat back on my haunches and pulled moss from my hair. "Seriously?"

"We need to move. Now." He picked up the other two weapons.

"Wait," I said. "There are two more. We don't know where they are."

"Exactly. But they know where we are. Now move."

"But we know they're headed this way, right?"

He glared at me. "Defensive tactical maneuver. We need to move."

I shook my head. "If we retreat, Maria will have time to get away, to alert others, to get rid of evidence, to—" I shook my head "—do other stuff. No way I'm giving her that chance."

Behind Dalton, a walking palm tree stood tall, its multitude of roots reaching out in many directions. I pushed past him, grabbed hold of a root, and shinnied upward, hand over hand, until I was about twenty feet off the ground.

"What the hell are you doing?" Dalton said in a whisper shout.

I surveyed the surroundings. The foliage was thick, but I thought I caught sight of movement about fifty yards out. I zeroed in. There it was again. A bird. Nothing. I slid back down the tree.

"I don't see anything," I said. "The other two must be with her."

"We don't know that," Dalton said. He quickly checked the other weapons for rounds. One was empty, the other had two left. He handed it to me and tossed the empty one into the green abyss.

"It makes sense." I looked at the three men tied up on the ground. They weren't trained guards. They probably didn't even know how to aim their weapons. I held the old, tape-covered rifle out in front of me. "You weren't shot with one of these," I said. "They sent these guys out to—" My eyes met Dalton's and simultaneously we said, "scare us off."

"What the hell's going on? Back at the shed, that guard recognized you." Dalton said. He put his hands on his hips and eyed me up and down.

I glanced over my shoulder, stalling.

"C'mon, Poppy. What's going on? You obviously know a lot more about this whole operation than you let on."

"Me? You're the one who was sleeping with her."

He glanced over his shoulder.

"Quit stalling," I said.

"Hey, she came on to me. I had to see where it would lead."

"And?"

He shrugged. "And I got nothing, okay?" He looked around again. "Other than she's kinky as all—"

"I got it," I said. I stared at him for a moment. What was I feeling? I mean, he could sleep with whomever he wanted. And the fact that he was joking right now, well—I shook my head. Despite the danger, or maybe because of it, he was enjoying this—the thrill of the chase, the undercover con, the adrenaline high. He was a junkie like me. And being hit on by a beautiful woman like Maria must have been—"Wait, why would she seduce you?"

He raised his eyebrows in an arrogant, macho, have-you-not-seen-my-pecs expression.

I slapped him on the arm.

"Ouch!" His hand jerked up to cover the wound.

"Oh, sorry," I said. "Maybe to see if you'd cheat on me? If so, maybe you'd be a crook, too. Then why use it to pit us against each other?"

"I'd been trying to figure that out." He squeezed his shoulder tighter. The wound was hurting. "Then yesterday, you were mad at me, so I went to see if George wanted to play a round of golf. He wasn't there but Maria invited me in." He wouldn't look me in the eye.

"Is that when you decided to take me to dinner?"

"Well, that's not—"

"Forget it," I said.

"Something was hinky about the whole thing. She was fishing for how I was feeling about you. I couldn't put my finger on it at the time. But just now, in the shed, I realized—"

"She saw us run into Noah at the fundraiser. She was trying to figure out if he and I—"

"Were having an affair."

So she did know about Noah being an activist. But does she know I was the one behind the whole Carlos takedown?

Dalton bore down on me. "What was that with the monkey?"

I clenched my teeth together. *Can't cry now. Focus.*

Dalton threw up his hands. "What am I saying? It doesn't matter. Our cover's blown."

"That's not...exactly true," I said.

He glared at me. "What does that mean?"

"She doesn't know we're cops. She thinks we're activists. Eco-terrorists." I gave him a please-don't-be-too-mad-at-me grin. "At least, she thinks I am."

"Dammit it. I knew it. Because of that Noah guy."

"Yeah, no. Maybe." I searched my brain for insight.

Something. "She was testing us, right? To see if we were activists or really potential buyers"—*that's it!*—"She still brought us *here*."

"That doesn't make sense."

It all made sense. She must have thought of the gang as a nuisance more than any serious threat. They'd been here before, several times. But Noah had only ever targeted the shed. She used the shed as a temporary shelter, one they could use to show animals, but was easily emptied. If she confirmed we were activists, no harm done. If we were buyers, she could have some class I species brought in for us to see. The guard had been about to hand her a two-way radio. That meant they were nearby. Perhaps she's always had them nearby. I looked at Dalton. "I can't explain right now but…I think I can still get what we came for." I looked over my shoulder. "You're gonna have to trust me."

He shook his head. "Do I have a choice?"

"Follow me."

He took a step and faltered.

"Let me look at that," I said.

He didn't want me to, but I pulled up his pant leg. The bullet had grazed his leg and left a gash in the side of his calf. When I looked up, he was looking down at it with an annoyed expression. He started to take off his shirt.

"I think it will take more than that," I said.

He rolled his shirt, then tied it around his leg above his knee. I snapped off a branch from the walking palm tree, broke it at the right height, then shoved it under his armpit—a make-shift crutch.

Now, with his shirt off, I could see the wound at his shoulder. A bullet had penetrated his chest just below his shoulder. Blood oozed from the wound. "That's not good," I said. "You need to sit down, sit still."

"I'll be fine," he said. "Now go."

"But—"

He had a look on his face like I was insulting him.

I shook my head. SEALs.

I darted through the jungle, heading toward the edge of the clearing. I came to a halt where I could see the horses.

"Still there," I said to Dalton as he came up behind me. "All three."

He nodded toward the shed. The two guards were at the doorway, eyes searching the forest. "So are they. I don't get it. She has two guns guarding an empty shed."

"Exactly." I turned to him. "Ever hear of the shell game?"

CHAPTER 20

We emerged from the foliage at the edge of the ravine where the cable stretched across to the other side. It was fastened to a tree above our heads. The basket hung on the far side. "She's over there," I whispered. "I think the class I species are too."

Usually there would be a rope to pull an empty car from one side to the other so a passenger could board from either direction. On this one, the rope was missing. Seemed Maria didn't want anyone sneaking up behind her.

I had to get across.

The rocky edges of the ravine were too steep or ragged to traverse. The cable was the only option. I craned my neck out to have a look. At the ravine's lowest point, the cable was about sixty feet above the ground.

"Give me your belt," I said.

"Are you doing what I think you're doing?"

"Give me the belt."

"She could be watching. She'll shoot you off that wire like a dove."

"Yeah," I held out my hand for the belt. "If she's watching."

He thought a moment, holding his shoulder. "I'm going with you."

"We only have one belt."

"I don't need a belt."

"You're injured. You could make it worse. I need you to

secure this side so I have a safe retreat. Besides—" I looked him up and down "—your pants might fall down."

I could tell, he was thinking of objections.

"You know I'm right."

He unclipped his belt and handed it to me, but before he let go of it, he looked me in the eyes. "Be careful." He raised the weapon. "And let me get into position to cover you."

I nodded, took the belt from him, and paused, eyeing him. A thought niggled at the back of my mind. "Stan said you could never connect George to a sale—no emails, no phone calls, whatever. But you were sure he was involved somehow because of intel you gleaned through a smuggler you'd nabbed, right?"

Dalton nodded. "Yeah, all the information he gave us panned out so far."

"Cell service is sketchy in the valley. I assume that's why George and Maria have a landline at the house. You've monitored that and George's cell phone, right?"

He nodded. "And we got nothing."

"Did you ever check for a mobile phone for Maria?"

"I think we checked. I mean, it would have been standard procedure. I don't remember there being one registered under her name." He shook his head, frustrated. "We never thought of her as a possibility."

I looked across the ravine. The hill sloped upward from where the cable car landed. There was probably good cell service up there.

I looked up at the cable and drew in a long, strengthening breath. *I have to get that phone.*

"Just confirm they're there, then get right back over here," he said.

I looked him in the eye. "Right. Intel. Not evidence."

He winced. For a moment, I thought it was from my comment, but he shifted and I could see he was in pain.

"You're going to hold the line, right? You'll stay awake,

right?"

He barely nodded.

"Dalton, don't you flake out on me. Keep hold of that weapon."

"I got it," he groaned. This time from annoyance. *Good.*

I climbed the tree to the cable, wrapped the belt around my waist and over the cable, and fastened the buckle. I tested my weight. It held. I pushed off from the tree, wrapped my legs around the cable, and pulled myself out into the open and paused. If she was watching and ready to shoot, she'd do it now.

Nothing.

I leaned back and, hand over hand, pulled myself out and over the ravine. The cable dipped with my weight. One hand, pull, other hand grab, pull, grab, pull, and I was across. I unhooked the buckle and dropped to the ground. I looked back. Dalton was watching me. I gave him a thumbs up and ducked into the cover of the trees.

A narrow path led upward toward the top of the ridge. Maria couldn't be far. Taking the path was too big of a risk and I had to be careful. I decided to parallel it through the thick jungle. I shoved my way through vines and branches, trying not to make any noise. It took me five minutes to get twenty-five feet. And I was soaking wet. Not to mention the threat of snakes. This wasn't going to work. Not without a machete. And a silent one at that. I had to take the trail after all.

I crept on hunter's feet. The trail meandered through the forest at a low uphill grade then turned and shot upward over rocky terrain, slick with the perpetual wet of the rainforest. There was no wind or rain to mask the sound of my footsteps. Just the buzz of insects and the occasional cackle of jungle birds. I took my time, cautious at every turn. She could be waiting for me, could be poised, ready with a gun.

The trail cut back, heading yet upward through a copse of bamboo. The forest was quiet here. I carefully placed each footstep, inching through to the other side. I stopped a moment. What if she hadn't come this way? What if this was all a diversion too, and I was missing something? Maria had proven to be sharp and devious. To bring Clyde was—no, I couldn't let my mind go there. *She's here. I know it.* I moved forward. I was getting closer; I could feel it.

The choking foliage of the jungle started to thin. I was reaching the top of the ridge.

The closer I got, the more it made sense. Maria could easily slip away under the guise of a leisurely horseback ride, hike up to this ridge, and without anyone listening, make calls, send emails. When I'd seen her a few days ago, at 11:30 at night, she could have been up here to call a contact in China or Indonesia. No one would know.

My heart started to pound faster. Everything would be on that phone.

I stepped around a banyan tree and saw movement. I ducked back to the cover of its thick trunk. About one hundred yards ahead, the path went under an enormous rock ledge, a natural overhang. On this end, a waterfall trickled from a tiny stream above. Beyond that, several cages had been built beneath the rock ceiling, protected from the blistering sun and rain. Explained why I hadn't seen it on Google Earth.

It looked like a trailside menagerie where one might stop and buy a handful of grain from an old gumball machine to feed the animals. The cage frames were crooked and hodgepodged together, built on makeshift risers. The sides were wrapped in chicken wire or chain link fencing or both. There were at least eight I could see. From this angle, it was difficult to discern what was in the cages, but in two I could easily see the bright red of scarlet macaws. The cage on the far end was built on the ground and large enough for a jaguar.

I took a step out from behind the tree to see further down the ledge. There was Maria. On the phone. She was pacing, chattering away. I couldn't make out the words over the trickle of the waterfall, but the tone of the conversation was not a happy one. She waved her hands in the air, making demanding gestures as she talked. Her little dogs lay in a patch of sun, snoozing. She yanked the phone from her ear and stood with her hands on her hips, fuming.

I pressed against the tree and clutched my shaking hands together, willing them to stop. I breathed in. Breathed out. My heartbeat started to return to normal. I took another long, soothing breath, letting the adrenaline dissipate through my bloodstream, then peeked from behind the tree again.

Maria had dropped her hands as though resigned to something. She stepped toward the cages and, I noticed now, a large cabinet tucked between them. She opened the hinged door and dragged out a bucket with a scoop. She surveyed the cages with an attitude of disgust. Must be Carlos usually fed the animals here. She set down the bucket and fiddled with the latch on a cage. This was my chance.

While her back was to me, I crept up behind her.

She shook some food into a bowl and slammed the door shut. "Animal sucio," she grumbled. *Filthy animal.*

"You're under arrest," I said.

She paused for a microsecond, then shrugged without turning around, as though she had known I was there. The dogs leaped from their naps, yipping and yapping their annoyance. "By whose authority?" she asked as matter-of-fact as if I'd asked her the time of day.

"U.S. Fish and Wildlife service, in coordination with Costa Rican authorities."

She turned to face me with an amused grin. "And what exactly am I being charged with?" Her eyes narrowed. "Because I'm certain I didn't make an offer to sell you anything."

"No," I said. "I'd have to have proof of that anyway, which I don't. But you know that."

She shrugged and turned her back on me.

"It is, however, illegal to have a class I species in your

possession."

She smirked at me over her shoulder. "A slap on the wrist. You'll get a bigger scolding for dragging me in." Her lip curled into a half grin. "That is, if you're really a cop."

I simply stared at her, giving her time to ponder.

She looked me up and down. "And you think you can take me in?"

"You could go willingly."

She huffed.

"Either way, with testimony from your brother Carlos, I think—"

She spun around. "Carlos has nothing to say." The dogs started yipping again.

"Oh, I don't know," I said. "He spent last night in jail facing charges for drug trafficking. He might be in a mood to deal."

Her eyes narrowed. I could see her mind racing. "¡Silencio!" she snapped at the dogs. *Hush!*

I grinned with satisfaction. "But even if he doesn't," I said, "if I arrest you on the minor charge, we have probable cause to check all items in your possession." My eyes dropped to her pocket where she had stuffed her phone.

She was smart enough to know she had all the evidence we needed right there to put her away for a very long time. Her nose twitched as if she'd smelled something rancid. Her eyes darted toward the trail behind me. I was right.

Then something in her demeanor changed. It was subtle. A confidence she didn't have a moment ago. She took a step toward me. "You think you're so clever. You have no phone, which means you haven't called for backup. Assuming you are a cop, like you say you are, you're undercover, so nobody knows you're here. Your partner was hit. Am I right? You're all alone. Young and desperate to make a bust." She paused. "You could just"—she waved her hands in the air—"disappear."

I steeled my gaze. "So could you." I shrugged and gave her a curt smile. "Then I could take over. After all, you've gone to a lot of trouble to hide your identity. No one knows who you are, right?"

She threw her head back and laughed, then she lunged at me with more force than I was expecting and knocked me to the ground. She took a step to run and I swiped her ankle with my hand. She stumbled and I was on my feet. I pounced on her back, slamming her against the cages. The birds fluttered and squawked. A howler monkey shook a door and bellowed at us. The dogs shrieked, scratching at my legs.

She spun around and grabbed me by the hair and yanked my head back. I brought my arm around and down hard on her elbow. As she let go, I rammed my forearm upward and slammed into her throat. She rammed her knee into my gut, knocking the wind out of me. That ticked me off.

I reared back and slapped her, open-handed right across the face. *Take that, bitch.* She tried to hit me back, but I deflected her arm and twisted, pinning it against her chest. She twisted somehow and we fell to the ground. I managed to get on top of her and she bucked beneath me. With the downward motion, I head-butted her right in the nose. I pulled back. Blood ran down her cheek. "That's for trying to steal my husband."

She tried to roll over on her side. I rammed my knee into her kidney. She groaned. I got to my feet. "Go ahead. Get up," I said.

She looked at me skeptically, assessing me, wondering, I'm sure, what I intended to do.

"C'mon, get up."

She rubbed blood from her nose.

"Get up!"

She got on her hands and knees, then slowly raised herself up to her feet.

"You're not a real cop," she said.

"Did I show you a badge?"

I saw a dawning awareness in her eyes, an awareness that she had completely misjudged me, followed by a gathering fear.

"Who the hell are you?"

"Doesn't matter. What's important is how much I know about you. I know you're a ruthless thug," I spat at her. "You torture and kill animals for money. With no remorse."

"Don't give me that righteous crap." Her lip quivered, ever so slightly.

"I'll give you my fist." I punched her in the face. She reared back. "And my foot," I said as I kicked her in the knee. She dropped to the ground. I grabbed hold of her by her hair and dragged her toward the big cage. As I shoved her inside, she grabbed hold of a poker stick that was propped against the side and swung it at me. Her arm couldn't extend enough to make any impact. I grabbed hold of her arm and reached for the door and slammed it shut, right on her wrist. She cried out in pain. "That's for Clyde." The stick dropped from her grip.

I snatched the phone from her hip pocket, slammed the door shut, and clicked the latch into place.

I leaned with my back against the cage and, after I caught my breath, fired up the phone. "What's the password?" I asked her.

"Go to hell," she growled.

The dogs whined at my feet. I reached down and picked one up. "You poor little orphan," I said, just to stir her up. I opened a cage and let out two scarlet macaws. Beautiful birds. Most people think of them as the iconic parrot. I watched them soar away in a flash of red, yellow, and blue. I put the dog in the cage, picked up her other dog, and put him in, too.

"Let them out!" she screamed.

I picked up the poker stick. The end had been whittled to a sharp point. "What's the password?" I shoved it between the bars and poked her in the shoulder. "You filthy animal."

She cried out. "Screw you!"

"I see," I said. "You want to play the guessing game." I plopped down, crossed my legs, and fiddled with the phone like a kid with a puzzle. "Your little pups have names. What did

George call them, Frick and Frack?"

She glared at me.

"Wouldn't be George. I mean, you don't really love him, right?"

She turned and wouldn't look at me.

"But Carlos. Tu hermano. Now there's definitely some love between you, no?" Her head swiveled around. "Ah, now we're getting somewhere. What was it that he called you? *Mariposa*?" I purposefully enunciated, emphasizing the proper pronunciation in Spanish. She winced. "M-a-r-i-p-o-s-a." I typed in the letters and the main screen came up. "For a big shot smuggler, you're not so bright," I said, shaking my head at her. I pulled up her email account and scanned through it—her contact list, her accounting files. "Tsk, tsk. Tú eras una niña muy traviesa." *You have been a very naughty girl.* I looked up from the phone. Her eyes were filled with rage. "You better get used to living in a cage."

CHAPTER 21

Sirens came roaring from the valley, first police, then the ambulance. The two remaining guards ditched their weapons and fled into the jungle. Dalton and I came out into the open to greet Nash.

I stood back and let Dalton do the talking while I chewed my thumbnail into a bloody mash. I hadn't exactly followed procedure. Or the line of command. Or the law. I switched to the other thumb.

Dalton was too stubborn to go in the ambulance until he'd told Nash everything. The shoulder wound needed immediate attention. He'd be taken directly to the hospital and into surgery right away, the paramedics told me. They paced. I paced with them.

Finally, he gave in and I watched the ambulance bump down the two-track driveway and disappear.

"We've got a lot to sort out here," Nash said to me. "But you two did a fine job."

"Thank you, sir." Hm. What exactly had Dalton told him?

"Do you have anything to add?"

I was tempted to tell him about Felix, to look for his body nearby. But the investigative team would search every inch of the grounds anyway. "No, sir." I hesitated. "If you don't mind, though, I do have a request."

Nash regarded me with curiosity. "Go ahead."

"The dogs, sir. I know a good home, someone who would love them. May I?"

He shrugged. "I supposed they'd end up at the local shelter anyway."

"Yes, sir."

"Get some rest." He eyed my tangled hair. " You look like hell."

"Yes, sir." I scooped up the dogs, put them in their saddle bags, mounted the horse, and headed back toward the house and the car.

As I rode, I thought of how I was going to tell Isabella about Clyde and the tears finally came. Poor Clyde. He had looked at me with those sad eyes, pleading for my help and there was nothing I could do. Maria might as well have ripped my heart from my chest for the hole that was left. I had filled it instantly with self-preservation, then rage. But now, there was nothing but an emptiness, an ache for the innocence of one little monkey. *What do I say? How do I explain?*

By the time I got to the horse barn, I had found my resolve. I didn't know quite how, what words I'd use, but I was going to tell Isabella he had been brave, that he died saving me.

I went straight to the tree house. The sun ducked below the horizon as I drove up. I let the dogs run free and they scampered along at my heels. A fire was crackling in the pit, four silhouettes encircling it. As I got closer, I could see it was Isabella, Noah, Claudia and Matt.

I stopped and drew in a deep, calming breath.

The dogs romped ahead.

Noah stood when he saw me, waving hello, a smile spread across his face, but I went straight to Isabella and wrapped my arms around her.

She knew. I didn't have to say anything. "Di' you get her?" was all she said.

I nodded. Her muscles relaxed as the tension left her body. I held her tight. Finally, she pulled away from my embrace. "I'm okay," she said. "I knew when her man show up at The Toucan and he want Clyde. I knew."

Claudia softly said, "Are these her dogs?"

"They need a good home now. I was hoping maybe…"

Isabella scooped one up and hugged it tightly. I smiled.

Claudia grinned and gave me a supportive nod. "Let's go get them some water," she said to Isabella. She grabbed Matt by the hand and tugged him along, leaving me alone with Noah.

He'd been watching without comment. Once they were out of earshot, he said, "That was really cool." He gave me a reassuring smile. "She'll give them lots of love."

"I know."

He turned his hazel eyes on me. The flickering firelight made them look like they were on fire. We both sat down in the sand.

"I'm sorry you got arrested," I said. "I couldn't risk my cover to—"

He held up a hand and shook his head. "I would do it again," he said. "But"—his eyes fell on my lips and I felt a surge of desire—"you do owe me one thing."

"Yes?" I managed, trying to keep the quiver from my voice.

He leaned toward me. "Your real name."

I grinned. "Poppy."

He smiled wide. "Seriously?"

"Special Agent Poppy McVie."

"It's nice to meet you, Special Agent Poppy McVie. Noah Kingston."

He kissed me, a long, passionate kiss. Then he sat back. "What now?"

I curled my lip. "I have to leave tomorrow. Back to Michigan."

His eyes got that then-we-have-all-night look. But I couldn't stay, not with Dalton at the hospital. "What about you?" I asked. "What will you do now?"

He eyed me with a thoughtful resignation. "I don't know.

Once the gang leaves for the season, and I no longer have to keep watch at the shed, I'll get pretty bored, I imagine. I was thinking maybe I'd join the Sea Shepherds," he said. "What do you think?"

I laughed. "Yeah, that's just your style."

We sat together by the fire for a while before the others began showing up. Once the whole gang was there, I told them about Maria and the take down, as much as I could reveal.

"Hear, hear!" someone said and the conversation turned to new adventures.

It didn't feel right to say goodbye. I'm like my father; he never accepted goodbyes. As we traveled, whenever we made new friends, he always wanted to believe we'd see them again. Instead of goodbye, he'd say happy trails and fade off into the sunset.

I gave Noah a kiss on the cheek, and when he went for more beer, I slipped away from the fire. Happy trails my smoking-hot-set-my-pants-on-fire friend, I thought. Perhaps our paths will cross again.

I fell asleep in a hard plastic chair in the waiting room. Sometime during the night, a nurse led me to the recovery room where I watched Dalton sleep for a while. His shoulder was bandaged with a mountain of gauze.

Finally, at 8:07 a.m., his eyelids fluttered and he looked around the room, taking in his surroundings. When his eyes found me, he relaxed and managed a smile. He muttered something.

"Don't try to talk," I said. I took his hand in mine and squeezed. "Go back to sleep."

His eyes drooped and gave in.

Two hours later, he awoke, bright eyed. A few hours and lots of paperwork after that, the doctor said I could take him home.

I drove toward the bungalow, but decided some fresh air and a nice view sounded much better. I picked up a take-out lunch, turned into the park, and took the short road to an overlook where I parked and we got out.

With the cool ocean breeze in our faces, we walked to the edge and peered out at the sea. A magnificent frigate bird soared overhead. Waves rolled in and lapped on the rocky beach below and the cry of the gulls echoed in the distance.

As soon as we sat down at a picnic table, I heard chittering. From the top of a palm, perched in the crook of a frond, a white-faced capuchin sat, eyeing our sandwiches.

"Look at him," I said.

Dalton smiled. "Right where he's meant to be."

His phone rang and he tried to answer it with his left hand. I clicked it on and held it to his ear until he could comfortably take it from me. He nodded, agreed, nodded some more.

I went back to the car, got my binoculars, and scanned the ocean while I waited. Far out from shore, I spotted dolphins playing in the waves.

Finally, Dalton disconnected. "That was Nash," he said. "Maria's phone was the mother lode. She had connections we had no idea about. Nash is downright giddy."

"That's great," I said.

"He says that because she ran her business so secretively and mostly via email, he's going to be able to step into her role, see who he can identify up the line. He's going to offer George a plea deal to keep him in place as the front man."

"What do you mean by step into her role?"

"He'll keep her business going exactly as she has been to draw out a bigger fish."

"So he'll actually keep selling and smuggling animals?"

He sighed. "Yes, sometimes that's what we have to do."

My hands tightened into fists. "But that's not right."

Dalton stared at me with a blank face. He was exhausted, too tired to argue.

I sat down at the picnic table across from him. "You're saying we did all this for nothing?"

"Of course not. As long as there is wildlife trafficking somewhere in the world, we need to infiltrate wherever we can. We've arrested Maria, she'll get her punishment, but it's all about supply and demand. As long as there's demand—"

"For the right price, someone will be happy to supply." I sighed.

"We took Maria out and we got Nash in. That's huge."

It had been our objective. But it didn't feel like a victory.

"You and I both know the problem is cultural," he said. "In the west, people want their own one-of-a-kind pet, something exotic that no one else has. It's all about status, elitism, whatever. And in the east, there are those who believe eating crushed rhino horn or shark fin soup will make them more virile. It's human nature. Only science and education will change it. It has to come from the top. Better laws. That takes time. Lots of time."

"And meanwhile?"

Dalton sighed. "Meanwhile, you and I keep the wolves at bay."

I frowned.

"Yeah, pardon the old saying. That's an insult to wolves."

At least we agreed on that.

We looked out at the ocean for a while.

"One more thing," Dalton said. "The nurse said the butterfly gardens received an anonymous donation for $200,000 on their web site. She said it was front page news. Know anything about that?"

I shook my head. "Not a clue."

"Uh-huh."

I tried to think of something else to say, but nothing seemed honest enough. My eyes dropped to the bandages taped across his chest and shoulder. "I should have told you earlier what was going on."

"It's okay."

"You weren't exactly straight with me either, you know. Sleeping with Maria. Is that even allowed?"

"I wasn't exactly going to spell it out in the report."

"But you already suspected her. No wonder you were so frustrated with me showing up."

He wouldn't acknowledge it.

"I'm sorry you were saddled with me, you know, a probie agent."

He flashed a smile. "I don't mind babysitting."

I kicked him under the table.

He laughed. "Actually, I think of you more as a little bundle of bad ass."

I laughed with him. It felt good. "Where will you be headed now?" I asked.

"Nash mentioned an op in Norway. Beautiful country." He seemed pensive. Maybe he wasn't allowed to share the details. "What about you?"

"I'm headed back to Michigan. I have a few weeks left of my field training." I still wasn't quite sure what Dalton thought of me. I sat up straight. "I busted a couple of rednecks taking a live bear the day I got called to Special Ops. My SAC got to catch the bastard they were selling to without me."

"Yeah, well, I'm sure he's anxious to have *you* back."

I shrugged. "He says I'm giving him an ulcer."

Dalton threw his head back and roared with laughter.

"Hey, it's not that funny," I said with a grin.

His eyes settled on mine and for a moment I saw the kind, loving eyes of the man who had held me while I cried, who had kissed me so tenderly. He held my gaze, then turned away.

"Well, hey, Norway. Wow." I reached for my sandwich. "I'm super jealous."

With his one good hand, he fidgeted with his sandwich wrapper.

I opened it and tucked the sides for him so he could hold it like a fast food burger. "Don't you want to go?" I asked.

"Oh yeah, I want to go. It's just, the cover needs to be just right, you know, to get approved."

Something in Dalton's expression made me feel uneasy.

He turned to face me and with a sigh of resignation, he said, "Nash says I have to take my wife."

Thank YOU for reading. If you enjoyed Poppy McVie and you feel as strongly as I do about the issues presented in this book and want to help, PLEASE start by taking a moment to post a review on Amazon.com or Goodreads.com
I would be grateful.

AUTHOR'S NOTE

Wildlife trafficking is estimated at over $20 billion annually and is rivaled only by illegal drugs and weapons in the money it earns criminals. The number of organized crime syndicates profiting from large scale trafficking is mind blowing. Millions of wild animals are captured and slaughtered each year for traditional medicine and aphrodisiacs, exotic pets, souvenirs and religious trinkets.

This cruel holocaust MUST STOP.

To help, 100% of the profits from the sale of this book will be donated to an organization fighting to protect wildlife. Each year, the organization will be chosen by you. Your vote counts! Go to: http://www.KimberliBindschatel.com/vote/ to vote today.

If you'd like to learn more and stay informed, please follow my blog at http://www.KimberliBindschatel.com

THANK YOU

Writing a novel is a huge endeavor and certainly not a solitary one. I am grateful so many people were willing to lend a hand.

Special thanks to Professor David Favre of the Animal Law Center at MSU for all the advice and guidance. Any error is mine alone.

Many thanks to Larry Richardson for helping me with some details about the U.S.F.W.S. To Jane Whaley for the juicy details in our interview. To Joel for the info on making a snake vomit. (I'm still not sure I got that right.) And to Roaster Jack for the coffee tips, especially those old roasters.

To Rachel and Dan for the feedback, especially at the early, rough stage when all is gobbledygook and nothing makes sense.

I am so thankful for my readers—April, Diane, Tricia, Linda, Kathleen, Michele, Ellen, Joni, Mary, Laura, Valerie, Andrea, and Jan. Their feedback was not only helpful but uplifting.

Thanks also to Amy for help with my Spanish, April for the subtitle, and Barbara for the exhaustive list of copy edits.

As always, a special thank you to my loving and supportive husband who has loved Poppy since the day she sprouted into my head. And to my parents, for raising me with a love of nature.

Thank YOU for reading. Please take a moment to post a review on Amazon.com or Goodreads.com I would be grateful.

ABOUT THE AUTHOR

Born and raised in Michigan, I spent summers at the lake, swimming, catching frogs, and chasing fireflies, winters building things out of cardboard and construction paper, writing stories, and dreaming of faraway places. Since I didn't make honors English in High School, I thought I couldn't write. So I started hanging out in the art room. The day I borrowed a camera, my love affair with photography began. Long before the birth of the pixel, I was exposing real silver halides to light and marveling at the magic of an image appearing on paper under a red light.

After college, I freelanced in commercial photography studios. During the long days of rigging strobes, one story haunted me. As happens in life though, before I could put it to words, I was possessed by another dream—to be a wildlife photographer. I trekked through the woods to find loons, grizzly bears, whales, and moose. Then, for six years, I put my heart and soul into publishing a nature magazine, *Whisper in the Woods*. But it was not meant to be my magnum opus. This time, my attention was drawn skyward. I'd always been fascinated by the aurora borealis, shimmering in the night sky, but now my focus went beyond, to the cosmos, to wonder about our place in the universe.

In the spring of 2010, I sat down at the computer, started typing words, and breathed life into a curious boy named Kiran in *The Path to the Sun*. Together, in our quest for truth, Kiran and I have explored the mind and spirit. Our journey has taken us to places of new perspective. Alas, the answers always seem just beyond our grasp, as elusive as a firefly on a warm autumn night.

Most recently, my focus has shifted to more pressing issues—imperiled wildlife. With the *Poppy McVie* series, I hope to bring some light into the shadowy underworld of black market wildlife trade, where millions of wild animals are captured or slaughtered annually to fund organized crime.

IT. MUST. STOP.

The adventure doesn't end for
Poppy and Dalton

Join them in Norway as they pursue a notorious
killer whale hunter in

Order it today on
amazon.com